THE VISIT

The Game on Thatcher Island
Friends
Transport 7-41-R

THE
VISIT

A NOVEL BY

T. DEGENS

THE VIKING PRESS
NEW YORK

First Edition
Copyright © 1982 by T. Degens
All rights reserved
First published in 1982 by The Viking Press
625 Madison Avenue, New York, New York 10022
Published simultaneously in Canada by Penguin Books Canada Limited
Printed in U.S.A.
1   2   3   4   5   86   85   84   83   82

Library of Congress Cataloging in Publication Data
Degens, T.   The visit.
Summary: At a family gathering in Berlin years after World War II,
Kate relives some of the events described in the diary of a dead
aunt who was once a member of the Hitler Youth.
[1. World War, 1939–1944—Germany—Fiction.
2. Germany—History—1933–1945—Fiction.   3. Aunts—Fiction] I. Title.
PZ7.D3637Vi   [Fic]   82-2600   ISBN 0-670-74712-2   AACR2

THE VISIT

ONE

◇ "Hitler did a lot of wonderful things," says my Aunt Sylvia, and I tick them off silently: building the superhighways, putting six million unemployed back to work, refuting the infamous Versailles Treaty. I study her; I search her face for clues to the past, for some kind of deformity that could have warned me: the thin white lines left by a scalpel, the skin transparent and stretched, that tell of attempts to erase or mask. But her face is wide and tanned and merry. There are crinkles of laughter around her pale blue eyes; her nose is humped like Dad's, the mouth full and mobile, the hair, still blond and curled, swept back. Only the cheeks hang heavy in velvet folds. It is a face I used to love. Yes, I did love it. Not long ago I loved and admired Aunt Sylvia.

I have to do it; my hands, taut and ice-cold, hold the gun as I pull the trigger. I listen to the bang, and I watch the bullet's impact. It hits Aunt Sylvia's forehead half an inch above her right eye. The skin dents and breaks. The bullet bores into the coat of flesh, tears it apart, and drills into the bone. The bone smashes and the skull rips open. Blood and brain and bone splatter. There are pink and white and gray exploding colors; they blur as I shake, nauseous. A great movie close-up, I try to think, but the fantasy sickens me, and I hide my hands.

Aunt Sylvia goes on talking.

"Imagine! Without a single shot Hitler rebuilt the German Reich, added the Rhineland, the Saar district, Austria, Czechoslovakia. By 1938 Germany was more powerful than ever before. Isn't it wonderful!"

This time she doesn't mean Hitler or Germany but the dish my mother is carrying toward the table. We are sitting on the patio, celebrating Grandma Hofmann's seventy-sixth birthday and Aunt Sylvia's once-a-year visit from Pasadena, California. She always stays a month. It is mid-September, and the weather is exceptionally fine, with the sun warming the brick walls and the sunflowers huge and nodding.

"Wonderful!" repeats my aunt in her accented German, eager, far too passionate. After all, it's only dessert.

It's Mom's specialty and traditional for this occasion. A bowl with layers of pound cake and Bavarian cream and praline and meringue, buried under whipped cream and surrounded by various fruits. It's a pretty good dessert.

Mom is serving, and I watch her. Her dark brown hair hides her face except for the tinted aviator glasses. I can't see through them, but I know her eyes are calm and friendly and just a bit mocking. Her mouth twitches a little. Mom is amused by a lot of things, and I do not understand all of them right away—like her laughter when my bike was stolen on Christmas Eve. Instead of jeans she is wearing an Indian skirt and blouse, and the long black fringe of the sleeve dips into her cup of coffee, into the sugar bowl, and back into the coffee while she is filling the plates. I know she'll laugh when she tastes her coffee; she hates it sweetened.

The first portion goes to Grandma, who is plump and

elegant in her gray silk dress. Grandma's tongue darts over her lips, and her cheeks quiver as she grabs for the plate. She loves sweets just as much as my brother, Nick, does.

Aunt Sylvia is given her plate, and she goes on talking in her exuberant voice; as always, the family yields to her flow of words without interrupting. She talks about how she misses German bread and German sausage and German family life and how she cherishes these afternoons all through the year—all of us sitting together around a beautifully decked table with its embroidered tablecloth, the matching napkins, the flowers, the heirloom china.

"Meissen, isn't it?" she says, and I remember the very same question from a year ago. It isn't Meissen; it's ordinary china, nothing exceptional, as she well knows.

Mom shakes her head, and Dad grins at his older sister. Except for the humped nose, they do not look alike. Dad's face is long and narrow, his beard and sideburns are brown, and he is quite bald. His eyes are deep-set and greenish, and the skin around them is smooth.

My brother, Nick, and I are served last. Craning his neck, Nick checks the plates and compares his share with the others. But Mom has been fair: his and Grandma's portions are by far the biggest.

I push mine toward my brother.

"I'll trade for . . ." I falter. I had not thought about it.

"You and your friends can listen to my records," he offers.

I wait for more. At fourteen Nick is rich. Sometimes he works after school, repairing bikes.

"I'll let you have my backpack for your next hike."

It's only fall, and the next hike is many months off, I think.

"Listen to *me*, Kate," cries Aunt Sylvia, interrupting with an offer of her own. "I'll take you to the zoo, the opera, the fairground. Or how about a helicopter ride over Berlin? You'll love it just as much as I do! It's a really wonderful experience!"

"The backpack," I say quickly to Nick. I know it is petty. Last year, when Aunt Sylvia stayed with us, I left my share of dessert on her bedside table.

Now I sit and make myself watch the blood stream down the side of her neck and seep into the lacy material of her dress. There are ugly wet blotches on her breast and stomach. I feel dreadful. I know I couldn't have eaten dessert anyway. There is a lump in my throat. I know that if it weren't for the notebook I would love Aunt Sylvia as I had before. It is hard for me not to love her.

But there is the notebook.

In May, when I was helping Dad search up in the attic for his graduation class picture—an anniversary was coming up—sifting through boxes with ancient letters, yellowed photographs, bills, travel folders, newspaper clippings, theater tickets, he gave it to me.

It was a child's notebook, slate blue, dog-eared, with black ink doodles on the cover. I don't think he had read more than a couple of sentences before he slumped back and stared silently into space till curiosity and impatience made me poke him.

"I don't know how this got here. It belonged to my sister Kate—your aunt—who died so long ago." His voice was the one he used when he read *Oliver Twist* or told us one of his dreams at breakfast. Right away I had thought of Aunt Sylvia, wondering brightly, as she did during every visit, why Kate wasn't with them any more, why she had to "go" so young, and Grandma Hofmann would say that it had been an accident, nothing but a terrible, terrible accident, and that the past was the past and should be left alone, or some such thing.

"I hardly remember her," Dad went on. "Maybe you should take care of the notebook." He handed it to me.

On the front page I read:

Diary of
KATHARINA LOUISE HELENE HOFMANN
Berlin
302 Spanish Avenue

It was my name and address.

I can still feel the sudden draft of cold air, the hairs on my arms and back rising, and my chest tightening. It was my name and address in an unfamiliar angular, firm handwriting. The first entry began June 23, 1943.

The other Kate had written years ago: "I can't wait for summer camp. Ten more days and I'll be gone!!!" The exclamation marks were straight, the last one as big as the page.

TWO

🖋 *June 23, 1943*

"Who has ever heard of Decherow!" cried Sylvia, bursting into the kitchen. "What a name! Some dump out in the sticks that nobody's ever been to. And that isn't the worst. Listen to this!" She paused, glaring at her audience—her mother, Sven Peter, Kate, and Belinda. They had been preparing the first harvest of strawberries for canning—cleaning jars, cutting up large strawberries, measuring out sugar. Now they dropped what they were doing and watched Sylvia brandishing her letter.

"But, Sylvia darling . . ." Her mother tried to soothe her, pulling Sven Peter on her lap.

"Blah . . blah . . blah . . 'July 3 till August 14, 1943, you will be assigned to Camp Decherow near the village of Decherow as cook. I know we can count on you to do your duty. Heil Hitler!' " Sylvia was mimicking the official tone to perfection; in fact, Kate thought she recognized the block warden with his slightly nasal twang.

"You should be proud to be trusted with a task like that." Her mother was reproving her gently. "It's an order, isn't it? Besides, you'll like the village, I'm sure."

"You should be camp leader," declared Kate. "Cook!

You're the worst cook I know. How come they picked you? Someone goofed.''

Sylvia flashed a smile at her sister. She took it as the compliment it was meant to be. Cooking was not on her list of priorities. That was for the likes of Belinda, the maid. Sylvia was going to be another Amelia Earhart, the world's most famous female aviator.

"Remember the chicken you roasted, guts and all? And you told us it was stuffed with spinach and terribly healthy. Some spinach!''

"The color was ghastly.'' Sylvia joined in. "What an atrocious greenish brown! And the smell—that was worse, wasn't it, Belinda?''

Stonily Belinda turned back to her canning.

"Sven Peter refused to touch it until I told him that was how the Eskimos ate their vegetables—right out of a reindeer's stomach.''

"Only chickens don't scratch for nice clean moss under the snow—they go after all sorts of garbage,'' Kate broke in, ignoring her mother's gasps.

"But you believed me, you and Sven Peter and Belinda! You ate the chicken and the stuffing!'' Sylvia's blue eyes sparkled.

"*They* believed you. I didn't for one single minute.'' Kate corrected her. "I ate it to prove to myself that I could do it. Just a test. Like letting a snail crawl up my arm or one of those fat white maggots pop in my mouth.''

Belinda knocked down a jar. It clanged on the tile floor and rolled under a cupboard.

"That's enough, Kate! Go to your room!'' Her mother's voice ruled out argument. Her sister winked at her, but Kate

9◇

saw that she, too, was upset. Sylvia's upper lip quivered.

So she ran upstairs and flopped on her bed.

It wasn't her room alone. She shared it with Belinda, one of a succession of mother's helpers who did their compulsory year of domestic service. Kate didn't mind. Some of the girls she had liked, some not. They didn't interest her that much. It was better than sharing the nursery with her little brother, Sven Peter, who was such a baby and still needed his afternoon naps. She thought it was only right that Sylvia was by herself in the blue room with the bay window across the hall. Sylvia was almost sixteen, in the ninth grade, beautiful and quite marvelous. That was why it was so puzzling that Kate hadn't come out with her news right away.

Kate burrowed under her mattress for the crumpled piece of paper and studied it again. Yes, there was no doubt about it; she, too, was signed up for Camp Decherow during the first half of Sylvia's reign in its kitchen, just as Kate had planned.

So why this wavering, as if she wanted to change her mind? When she had been told about camp at the Youth meeting on Saturday, she had felt weak with excitement and pleasure, and she had kept it a secret, to gloat over alone. Only this morning she had written in her notebook, "I can't wait for summer camp," and now for a second she wished she weren't going at all.

Kate shredded the paper and threw the pieces out the window. The house across the way, partially bombed a year ago, was hidden behind treetops. One of the chestnut trees had been split in half and was slowly dying. In the front yard she saw Sven Peter's tiny wooden scooter and the battered bike she had inherited from Sylvia.

I am happy that Sylvia and I will be together, she thought. That's what I wanted. But why wasn't Sylvia in charge of the camp? Surely she could serve the country better by doing more important work than cooking stews and washing dishes. Like chaperoning trainloads of little kids out of the city or helping in the hospitals with the wounded soldiers, even doing odd jobs at the glider hangar. Sylvia was so talented.

I'll tell her I'm going too, thought Kate. I'll tell her now. Through the window she could see Sylvia leaving the house, swinging her tennis racket.

"Have a good time," her mother and Sven Peter were calling from the steps. Then they returned to their strawberries in the hot kitchen, and Kate slipped down to follow her sister.

She trailed her along Spanish Avenue, past the turnoff to the tennis courts. Sylvia walked straight on, her mop of golden curls, tied with one of the fashionable black velvet bows, bouncing, sun and shadows playing on her white skirt and blouse. Two crossings later she entered the park.

Kate went after her. She trotted around clumps of rhododendron and through a bed of early sweet peas, and then knelt behind a stone bench and saw her sister break into a run and race toward the fountain. It looked like a hundred-yard dash that ended—like one of Sven Peter's darts across the lawn—in the outstretched arms of a grown-up person. He whirled her around just as her dad whirled Sven Peter when he was home on leave. Her little brother always squealed. So did Sylvia.

Kate drew in her breath sharply. She knew him. He was First Lieutenant Werner Grasshof, who had just been awarded the highest medal of honor for shooting down more enemy planes in the past couple of months than anybody else.

He was a hero.

On Friday he had addressed the school assembly, standing tall and erect and incredibly handsome on the platform, his left arm in a black sling. Dr. Ott had introduced him as the school's most famous alumnus, as they stood beneath the gigantic swastika, and the Führer staring pensively over the mass of students out of a golden frame of oak leaves, his hands clasped in front of him. Kate, seated among the sixth graders in the first row, had listened this time, instead of trying to memorize the lists of World War I dead, engraved on two large marble tablets. Adam, Brinkmann, Budenhagen, three Müllers, and on and on.

A live hero.

Even now she could quote nearly all he had said about the Fatherland and the need to stand close, shoulder to shoulder, to fight the enemy, young and old, one body, one mind, in the great fellowship of battle. And of the spirit that took hold of him when he soared high in his plane, invincible, daring the elements and the enemy, and how eager he was to go back, the wound healed, his arm as good as new. And the proudest moment in his life when the Führer, Adolf Hitler, had placed the medal around his neck.

"I've got to touch him," her friend Brenda had whispered to Kate.

"You're crazy!"

"Want to bet?"

Kate had examined her friend and decided to bet low.

Brenda had seemed quite determined, and with the stage only a few feet away, her chances were good.

"Two fliers," Kate had offered. Two out of her collection of enemy leaflets the British and the Americans dropped during their bombing raids, full of absurd lies. You were requested to deliver them at the Party offices, but all the kids she knew were avid collectors, and trading was hot.

"Okay." Brenda had focused her attention on the stage, and Kate waited uneasily. At times Brenda could be embarrassingly theatrical. Just like her sister.

It had turned out to be simple and natural, and probably lots of students in the assembly hall had felt a surge of envy. For the national anthem, First Lieutenant Werner Grasshof had stepped down among the kids in the center aisle. Brenda had needed only to lurch forward and faint, crumbling down his legs. With one arm he had picked her up and finished the song, holding her close, like a soldier carrying his wounded comrade, Kate had thought.

On the way out Brenda had put her arms around his neck and touched the medal. And on the way home Kate had held Brenda's hand and hadn't washed hers till nightfall.

And Sylvia had won him.

Here she was, being whirled around and around and then locked in a two-minute kiss that looked a lot more bearable than the one Karl Brand, the twelfth-grade javelin champion, had pressed upon Sylvia earlier that year. Then Kate had thought her sister's back would snap. Afterward, holding hands, Sylvia and the first lieutenant walked around the dry fountain, Werner Grasshof dangling the racket and the black sling. Obviously his arm was well and he would soon return to his unit. Kate heard their amused laughter. Nobody beats Sylvia, she thought, and she was proud of her sister.

Later that evening she went into Sylvia's room.

"I saw you in the park today."

"Fifty-one . . . fifty-two . . . fifty-three . . ." Sylvia was brushing her hair. She sat in front of her dresser with the triptych mirror. Kate liked the dresser, but she liked the desk better. It had belonged to her Great-grandmother Hofmann, and it was carved and polished cherrywood, with scores of drawers and pigeonholes and two known secret compartments. Now it was Sylvia's.

"Would you like to meet him?" Sylvia kept on brushing calmly.

"You mean it? You really do?" Kate was jumping up and down.

"Why don't you go to Herder's down at the lake? We'll be there tomorrow about four-thirty. Their ice cream is still pretty good."

Kate nodded. "Can I brush your hair?"

Sylvia settled back, and Kate began counting at one. At seventy-eight she paused. Her arm was aching, but she did not admit it.

"By the way," she said, watching her sister's face in the mirror, "I'm going to the same camp as you—Decherow."

"That's wonderful!" Sylvia smiled at her. Her smile was wide, delighted, in all three mirrors, and Kate felt again like jumping up and down.

"Any of your friends going?" Sylvia asked after a minute of silence.

Kate shook her head.

"Remember when you answered for me at the big rally?" Sylvia asked again.

"You were late, and with so many people nobody could tell it wasn't you," said Kate.

"And how about the time you handed in my geography drawings and got an A plus?"

Kate nodded. "I changed the S into K. That was easy."

"I picked you as my assistant for my mind-reading act at the hospital benefit, and nobody suspected we knew each other," Sylvia said.

"So we tricked them together!" Kate grinned.

"Remember when we both got hold of the special textile coupons? There was only one per family, but people didn't know we were sisters."

Kate did remember. Sylvia had told her to give a fake address. Hofmann was a common enough name. Her mother had been terribly pleased with the material, although Kate thought their three dresses ugly.

"Tell you what we'll do at camp," Sylvia said suddenly. "We'll pretend we don't know each other. It'll be much more fun—I'll depend on you, and you'll depend on me, and nobody will be the wiser. It's wonderful to have somebody you absolutely trust, Katie—it's really wonderful. But you must promise not to tell."

"You want us to swear by the propeller?"

It was their private pledge.

"Yes. Let's do it." Sylvia got up, her face solemn, and together they went downstairs to the living room.

"I swear I will not tell anyone at summer camp that we are related," Kate repeated quickly after her sister, and pulled her hand away from the wood. She was half convinced that the propeller her father had brought back from World War I and installed above the couch would slay her if she ever broke a promise. It was a ten-foot-long chunk of gleaming, shaped mahogany of considerable weight.

The next afternoon Kate peered through the windows at Herder's. There were wrought-iron tables and chairs, bulky ferns and dusty palms, black-tailed waiters, and a glass buffet with all sorts of cakes. Sylvia and her ace were not among the guests. It was four o'clock, and Kate paced back and forth, waiting. She was wearing her Hitler Youth uniform—white blouse, dark blue skirt, pea jacket. She knew Werner Grasshof would be wearing his. Her straight brown hair was braided, and she had tied the braids with brown ribbons instead of rubber bands.

It was a beautiful afternoon, warm and clear and nearly cloudless. Some kids were splashing in the lake, though the water would still be cool. Others were rowing, and Kate heard the barked commands. She watched a string of ducks swoop down. It would take them about three hours at a speed of ten kilometers per hour to fly across Berlin, the capital of the German Reich, she remembered her father explaining. He liked to put facts in aeronautical terms. He could do it in an Arado 96 in ten minutes, he said, with a loop above the Brandenburger Tor and hedge-hopping over the Reichskanzlei as a special reference to the Führer.

Kate waited till it was past suppertime.

At home Sylvia hailed her on the landing between the fire-fighting equipment, the pails with sand and water, the mop, the ax, the shovels. Kate was going up to bed.

"Gosh, Katie, I hope you didn't wait or anything. He offered to take me up in his plane. It was simply wonderful!

We flew east—we did all sorts of crazy things. I couldn't say no, could I? You wouldn't have wanted me to, would you?''

"Of course not!" It wasn't Sylvia's fault she had hung around Herder's for hours. "What did Mother say?"

"It's all very hush-hush." Sylvia put a finger on her lips. She was glowing with excitement. "I was flying, Kate! I was flying!"

Kate thought her sister would make a great pilot.

THREE

◇ Grandma and Aunt Sylvia are going up to the blue room. I tag after them with Bozo. Aunt Sylvia supports Grandma as they slowly climb the stairs. There is no longer any firefighting equipment on the landing, but a jungle of plants—rubber plants, ivy, aspidistra, African violets.

"The ugly ones never want to die," Mom always says when she waters them. Some were gifts, others came with the house. "Living fossils."

"Anne put up these pictures," says Grandma. On the wall hangs a sequence of stark seascapes in charcoal. Grandma purses her lips to show her dislike. Anne is my mother, and Grandma usually agrees with her, but she does not like changes in the house.

She and Grandpa bought it many years ago.

"And our little Sylvia in a white sailor dress came along when we bought it. She picked out the blue room for herself. And later on, whenever we tried to move her, she would throw a tantrum," Grandma remembers fondly. Aunt Sylvia still looks smug when she hears the story.

Grandma now lives on the ground floor on account of her arthritis, in what used to be Grandpa's study. She lives among large dark, well-polished furniture, knickknacks, photographs, and the smell of anise cookies.

"The old pictures were cheap prints of Greek and Roman ruins," I say.

Grandma sighs. "We all loved them. I saved them through the war. Child, I hope you will never have to learn what that means. But I fought to hold on to this house and everything in it. There were the bombing victims and the refugees who would try to steal the pillow from under your head. The air raids, the bombs, the Battle of Berlin, the Russians, and then the blockade! But I kept my home for my family," she ends fiercely.

"And we do appreciate it! Mother, you were wonderful," sings Aunt Sylvia. "And isn't it marvelous that Sven Peter was offered such a good job at the research lab that he could come back to Berlin, and the family can live together in the old home!"

My parents moved from Cologne to Berlin six years ago.

We cross the hall. I am glad I don't have the room to the left. Mine is on the third floor, with slanted walls and a dormer jutting into a huge chestnut tree. I had painted one wall myself with a Tarzan jungle mural. Nick kept harping on how the chimp was a perfect self-portrait. Now all walls are white. I do not share the room with anyone. Mom does not have a mother's helper. Instead Mrs. Malek comes twice a week to drink coffee, talk, and vacuum.

The room to the left is Mom's workroom. She does drawings for a construction firm. I don't think she knows it was Kate's room. Mom has nothing to do with its past. She is very vague about Dad's other sister.

"The family never encouraged talking about her. I think it's too painful for them," she said when I asked.

Aunt Sylvia throws her door open. "Come in and sit over here!"

It is here that I read the notebook last May. It is here that I thought about it. I would come up to Aunt Sylvia's room, lie on the mauve settee, the rug, or her bed, sit at her desk, in front of her mirror, lean out the window, watching a movie inside my head. I would lie and stare into space, and the reel would be spinning on. I know it's my version of what happened. I have only the other Kate's words and what I make of them. But for me it is enough.

Aunt Sylvia settles Grandma on the mauve settee. Bozo and I squat on the pillows that line the curved seat at the bay window. The leaves of the wild vine touch the window-pane. Their green is patched with reds and yellows. The vines are ancient and strong enough for Nick and me to climb them together. "I love this room," cries Aunt Sylvia. She looks at herself in the triptych mirror and repaints her lips. She strokes the desk and opens one of its drawers. She plumps the plump cushions on the bed. She glances at the pictures. One is a photograph of her on Grandpa's lap. Another shows her waving out of a cockpit, wearing a flying cap and goggles. There is a gorge and waterfall, done in oil. The wallpaper is still blue with a thin white pattern.

"We do keep it exactly the way you like it," declares Grandma. "I insist on it. It will always be here, ready for you."

Her eyes water.

Aunt Sylvia does not notice. She rummages in her suitcase. It is huge and covered with airline stickers.

Air Singapore, Philippine Airlines, I read. Aunt Sylvia is

a tireless traveler. Not by profession—for fun! Rarely does she arrive straight from California.

"The islands are lovely," she says. "Here is a native doll for you, Kate dear. I must have bought it in . . . well, it doesn't matter, it will come to me. A bit crude, don't you think, Mother? The natives are rather primitive."

"I'm no longer interested in dolls." I used to be quite a collector. "Give it to someone else."

Before Grandma Hofmann can send me to my room, I drag Bozo to the door.

"You can't *do* anything with that girl," I hear Grandma complain. "She is so negative!"

I have the reputation now of being a difficult adolescent.

FOUR

🌿 *July 3, 1943*

At 8:35 Kate stood on Platform 7 of Anhalter station in the center of Berlin. Her backpack was still neat with the mud-brown blanket rolled tightly and fastened to the top, but her Hitler Youth uniform was no longer faultless. There were gray smudges on the white blouse, a button was missing, the neckerchief askew, and part of the seam at the front of her skirt ripped. An easterly wind blew, warm and dry. It was going to be a hot day with a few large white clouds, and Kate was panting. Belinda, near her, was wiping her face. On her back and under her arms sweat had changed the color of her blouse to a dark pink.

Kate had said good-bye to her mother and Sven Peter at the gate of 302 Spanish Avenue, and her mother's last-minute advice followed her down to the next block.

"Don't forget to change trains."

"Be sure to go to the Zoo bunker if there's an air raid!"

"Brush your teeth and don't dawdle over breakfast."

"Give our love to Sylvia! Help your sister, do you hear me?"

Sylvia had gone ahead two days before, for training, preparations and provisions—or so she said. In the fourth year of the war rides were rare, yet a staff car had picked her up.

"Do you mind taking some of my gear along with you, Kate?" she had asked.

"Of course not! Why should she mind?" her mother had answered for her.

There were plenty of reasons to mind, thought Kate, kicking the offensive piece of luggage—a steamer trunk decorated with stickers from London, Paris, New York, Tokyo. She and Belinda had lugged it to the station. It was too heavy, it was too large, it was too opulent, it did not belong in a Hitler Youth camp. It was an embarrassment. Surely her mother had packed it after Sylvia left.

Kate looked around the platform. She wouldn't be the only camper from Berlin. There was a kid with glasses and a jade-green blanket strapped to her pack; another one with a much too long skirt. Three girls with neat uniforms and packs were talking together, and one of them wore the green rope of a group leader. Close to her a pair of pale, sharp-nosed twins perched on a bench. Their badges were sewn crookedly, their socks slipping. One even wore high-heeled pumps. Kate would have liked to join the three friends, but she felt tied to the trunk.

Now one of the twins came strolling over and circled the trunk.

"Hotel Martinique, Broadway and 32nd Street, New York," she read aloud. "Is that where you're going?"

Kate ignored her.

"Paris. That's where Uncle Paul is stationed. Paris, capital of France. Two million five hundred and sixty thousand inhabitants fell into German hands when the French surrendered on June 22, 1940,'' she rattled on. ''The Versailles Treaty . . .''

Luckily the train was pulling in and its noise drowned her. She stopped speaking, and her twin steered her away.

It was a slow, old-fashioned train; each compartment had its separate door. After the maneuver of loading the trunk, Kate lowered the window with its leather strap and called out to Belinda, ''Please don't forget to water my garden!''

Belinda was already halfway down the platform, and Kate knew she'd take her time before showing up at her mother's. Belinda always took her time. Kate's garden wouldn't survive.

The compartment was empty except for a thin-lipped old man and his shopping basket, and a woman and her small son. The old man complained about the draft, so Kate closed the window. She let it down again when he got out at the third stop. Now the woman frowned at her, so she hastily pulled at the sash. The boy stuck his tongue out.

The train chugged past the outskirts of Berlin and gained speed, traveling through pine woods, along tree-lined country roads and patches of heather. Then came fields, pastures, villages. When mother and son departed, a stocky, fresh-faced farmer's wife climbed in and flung a pair of roosters into the luggage rack before she settled back and unwrapped a hunk of bread, smoked bacon, and a knife.

The roosters lay there dead, their long necks, swinging like pendulums with the motion of the train. Kate could not help looking at the big birds, their perfect velvety brown feathers, their scaly legs, their claws, yellowish and well-worn like her grandfather's toenails, their eyes naked in spite of the thin blue lids. Then a weak crowing showed them to be alive. Kate felt sick with disgust.

"Take them down, please," she said. "It's horrible for them with their heads upside down. There's enough room next to me."

She edged closer to the window. There was plenty of room. The bench on her side was hers alone.

The woman stared back at Kate, impassive, as if she had been addressed in an unknown language, and then she took another bite of her bread. She chewed, untroubled, and Kate thought her eyes looked hard and cold and contemptuous within a jolly mask. She shivered.

"Please," she said once more. "Please take them down."

The woman cut off another piece of bacon and stuffed it into her mouth. Her jaws clamped shut and began to move. She had to be a foreigner, from Poland or the Ukraine, thought Kate, some primitive country where people didn't know any better.

At the next town the woman packed up and grabbed her birds.

"Don't let them upset you," she told Kate with a broad grin. "They feel nothing. They're only animals, aren't they?"

"Dumb bitch," Kate cried after her as she hustled along the platform, the roosters slung over her shoulders. The engine whistled.

One more hour of pines and birches, oaks and beeches, fields, meadows, clustered farms, small country towns, glimpses of lakes, wide-open sky. Kate leaned out of her window. Two cars ahead, one of the twins was hanging out of their window, waving. Kate waved back.

When the train reached Gatow, she saw a dirt platform, cluttered with metal milk cans and crates of vegetables, a rusty detergent ad dwarfing the station building, a bench with a couple of uniformed girls, one holding a flag; a stationmaster much too grand in his red cap for the puny station. Here she was going to change trains for Decherow.

She let the twins help her with the trunk, pushing it into the jumble of luggage. Then she looked for Sylvia. About twenty girls were milling around with their packs. There was the kid with the horrible jade-green blanket, the one with the long skirt, the three friends. No, her sister had not been able to meet the train.

"You can still get out of it," one twin whispered as the train rattled slowly forward. "It's your last chance to avoid camping."

"Why should I? Didn't you want to come?" Kate asked her, taken aback.

"Attention! Fall in for roll call!"

The girls scrambled to line up. Kate went to the rear of the column.

The girl in front was perhaps fifteen years old, tall, with a plain face and very large teeth and the calves of a runner. Her mousy hair was held in place by a silver band. She looked determined. Her uniform was neat, the black neckerchief straight, the insignia in place. The triangle above the swastika on her left arm read "Gau North Mecklenburg." So she wasn't from Berlin, Kate thought. She would know all the local plants.

"At ease! I am Maren Fischer, in command of Camp Decherow. I welcome you and expect we will work together successfully. There is no further transportation to Decherow except our own feet, so let's march. Any questions?''

"How far is it?''

"About four miles.''

Someone groaned; others laughed nervously.

"Couldn't we get a buggy?'' It was a twin who asked.

"Remember there is a war on,'' came the routine answer. "Don't you do any cross-country marching in your Berlin units?''

"It's my shoes I'm worried about,'' mumbled the twin. "We got bombed, and I'm wearing my mother's.'' She displayed her feet, and Kate had to grin. Black pumps! They were such improbable hiking shoes.

The girls turned right and, following Maren's shouted commands, marched toward the gate. Kate brought up the rear. Now they started to sing.

As the pair of girls ahead of her filed through the station building, Kate ran back. She pointed out the trunk to the stationmaster, asked him to look out for it, and before he could scratch his head or pull out his forms for her to sign, she was sprinting after her group. Only the talkative twin had noticed her absence, and winked. No longer hampered, Kate joined in the singing with a loud voice.

"Forward, forward, shout the shining fanfares, forward, forward, youth knows no dangers . . .'' It was one of her favorite songs.

Four miles in the hot midday sun on a potholed gravel road lined with meager pear and apple trees, past fields of wheat and rye and barley, potatoes and beets, were four very long miles for marchers loaded down with heavy packs.

"How can I go on with this!'' One of the three friends

peeled off her sock and revealed a large red blister. It was their first rest in the grass beyond the roadside ditch.

The one they called Marianne laughed and then recited the slogan of the Hitler Youth: "Quick as a greyhound, tough as leather, and hard as Krupp's steel," but Ose, the third of the group, took out her handkerchief to cushion her friend's sandal. The marching did not bother Kate. It was part of summer camp. Besides, her shoes fitted well.

"You aren't tired already, are you?" Maren teased them on. "Don't tell me kids from Berlin have no spunk!"

During the second rest stop Kate sprawled in the shade of a beech tree, sucking one of the scrawny sour apples. It was her dessert after they all had pooled their travel provisions. It had been quite a good lunch with sandwiches from so many different homes. Kate had liked the salami best, and the dried-up cottage cheese the least. There was a vast expanse of leafy sugar beets across the road, an endless field, and in a span of haze, far away, Kate saw a group of people. Lazily she counted six who were hoeing in a rapid steady rhythm while two more stood aside. Then she fell back and watched the sunlight in the tree above.

"Wake up, everybody! Time to go on!"

Maren was passing a box of lemon drops. Kate noticed the talkative twin take three openly while everybody else took one. By now she knew most of her companions. More than half came from various parts of Berlin, the rest from small towns south and north of it. Even Maren had never been near Decherow. She lived on the Baltic Sea, at Warnemünde. She told them how proud she was to command the camp and that she had planned their work and activities.

"Because we have to do our share in the war effort, and

we want to do it, don't we?" she said. But Kate was disappointed when she showed Maren the common coltsfoot and she identified it confidently as wild rhubarb. Maren did not know any botany, and yet she was leader of a camp that had as its main purpose the collection of plants for medicinal and other uses!

Kate decided that of all the girls she disliked Sigrid in the sloppy skirt the most; Sigrid smelled unwashed. She liked the three friends the best—Ose, because she had earned the most important sports badges, and Inga, because she could imitate bird calls. Marianne had two brothers in the air force and was going to lead her own group in the fall. The kid with the jade-green blanket, Trudy, couldn't even clear a ditch without stumbling. There was another girl, Frokke, who had brought the flag. She had small gray eyes and a stern, competent manner; she stayed close to Maren. And there were the twins.

"I'm Kriemhild and she's Brunhild. Our mother is a Wagner fan. You know, the great German composer, 1813 to 1883, who wrote operas," the talkative twin had said, while the other twin had looked pained. "I think she regrets it now."

Kate had thought of an oil painting in the air ministry—Kriemhild and her athletic companions, golden hair flowing, charging through a dark forest. So unlike the pale, colorless twins.

They were singing again as they followed the sign to the youth hostel, turning off the main road, when the first roofs of Decherow could be seen ahead. The new road, narrower now, led gently uphill between peas on one side and rye on the other, and into a forest. Beeches grew tall, their smooth bark silvery. The song petered out. One couldn't sing with a parched throat, Kate thought as Maren's voice alone held the tune. After half a mile the road dipped and there was the hostel in a wide clearing, a bright two-story building, doors and windows open, inviting.

Maren let them wait in formation under the flagpole while she went inside.

"I'll have an upper bunk," announced Kriemhild.

"Gosh, I'm thirsty!" said another girl.

Kate looked for Sylvia and wondered which window belonged to the kitchen.

Then Maren came back, her face flushed.

"They're filled up," she said, halting. "Yesterday they got a group with high priority—bombing victims." She paused as if looking around for help. "They didn't even know we were coming."

Suddenly doors and windows of the hostel were crowded with laughing, gesticulating boys and girls.

"We'll go to Decherow for instruction," Maren said, and headed for the line of trees. Breaking ranks, the group went after her. It seemed like a retreat, like running away, and Kate would have liked more order, a call for attention, a steady step.

Sylvia was right, she thought as they waited for Maren, who had gone in search of the local party official: Decherow was a dump. Crumbling barns, ramshackle farmhouses, weedy gardens, pigs and cows with a thick coat of dung. The village green had grass only in patches around the central pump and trough, and everywhere else was barren and dusty. There was a wilted wreath on a war memorial with a robust angel striding into space above two dying soldiers.

The girls piled their packs on the single bench. Shrieking, they splashed each other at the trough, gawked at by a bunch of barefoot village kids and their mangy dogs. As Kate raced after the twin, Kriemhild, with her mess tin full of water, she banged into a boy about her size. His face under a vi-sored cap was disfigured by a welt on his upper lip. A hare-lipped kid.

"Watch out!" she cried harshly, because he had upset her.

Maren had just returned, sweaty, her neckerchief crooked, looking somehow smaller, when a limousine, its standard flying, drove onto the green and screeched to a stop. A sol-dier opened the door to let out—Sylvia. Sylvia, beautiful in a cornflower-blue summer dress. She bent back for a fare-well. The engine started. She waved; a hand waved back. When the car had vanished between barns, she faced the group of girls. She must have seen her sister but gave no sign. With a fine instinct for who mattered, she reported to Maren.

And Maren did not question her but poured out their troubles.

"When I was in Greece with the Eighth Squadron, we requisitioned the buildings we needed." Sylvia's clear, sure voice rang across the green.

FIVE

◇ It is Sunday morning after church. Grandma Hofmann, in hat and veil, sits upright in the front seat of the car, and Nick yawns in the back. "Who is walking home with me?" Aunt Sylvia asks.

Bozo scrambles out of the car. He is my dog, but he ignores me when she is here. He licks her shoes.

"I know you love me, Bozo! How about you, Nick? Kate?"

Nick already stands next to her.

I nod sullenly.

"I'll come along," says Dad. He likes to walk. It's Aunt Sylvia's second day with us. Mom drives off to cook lunch. Mom doesn't go in for needless exercise; besides, she says, someone has to do the cooking.

I start out ahead. Behind me I hear Aunt Sylvia just as I heard her throughout the service. With a loud, exalted, ringing voice she led the congregation singing and praying. Grandma Hofmann used to give me twenty cents if she could pick out my voice in church. I don't earn it any more.

"This is fun, Kate!"

The horse chestnuts are nearly ready to drop. I look for a stick to throw and knock them down. Aunt Sylvia and Nick are faster.

"Watch out," she cries, and I watch her stick flying high into the tree. Leaves and chestnuts and dead wood rain down. Bozo chases after the lot.

"Good shot." Dad applauds his sister, and Bozo delivers more chestnuts.

We turn into the park. Aunt Sylvia keeps throwing the stick, and Bozo returns it, panting. The fountain is spurting, the basin full of water. Bozo drinks in hectic laps. He wheezes. He is too old and fat to run. I hide the stick between the tangled bodies of two nymphs.

"Go find the stick, Bozo. Go find the stick."

It is not Aunt Sylvia's fault her glove falls into the water and Bozo dives after it. He comes up with a crown of green scum. He makes the basin overflow, and we laugh.

"Isn't he wonderful," Aunt Sylvia says. "So obedient! Such a good dog."

Through a tunnel of rhododendron we pass into Spanish Avenue.

"Do we have time for a cup of coffee?"

On Sunday mornings after church during Aunt Sylvia's visits there is always time for a cup of coffee, a glass of beer, wine, champagne. Mainly champagne. And ice cream or Coke for me and Nick, although it will spoil our appetite for lunch.

We walk across the street and through a network of smaller roads with comfortable suburban houses to a restaurant above the lake. It isn't called Herder's any more; now it's Lakeview, and the marble-topped tables and palms and ferns are gone too.

Aunt Sylvia enters first and chooses a table at the window. There is a reserved sign on it, and the waiter removes it quickly. Everybody can hear her as she orders champagne, the best, and a bone for Bozo. The waiter beams. Aunt Sylvia always tips beforehand. She is generous.

"Strawberry sundaes for you two? Nick? Kate?"

Their sundaes are huge. Nick asks for one with a double helping of whipped cream.

"Nothing for me." I shake my head.

"Black currant juice for the young lady." Aunt Sylvia scrutinizes me. "You do look tired."

"I am not tired," I protest. I hate being told I am tired when I just got up. I know I sound sharp.

"Don't you know she was born crabby?" says Nick.

Aunt Sylvia, Dad, and Nick are chatting about sports. Aunt Sylvia is interested in tennis, Nick in bicycle racing, and Dad in football. I watch some kids splashing in the water, and the sailboats maneuvering across the lake. The pines on the other shore are a dusty green. Today I did part my hair the way the other Kate used to part hers. Now my scalp hurts dully. I pinch myself hard to feel something else.

Suddenly it is nearly lunchtime and we leave.

"Race you back to the house," cries Aunt Sylvia, and she and Dad and Nick take off, shouting. Bozo and I lag behind. This time I am not even trying to beat her. Aunt Sylvia is the only grown-up person I know who loves to race kids and does not mind losing. Anyway, today she loses to Nick but beats her own brother.

SIX

🌿 *July 4, 1943*

The moon woke Kate up. Moonlight was bright on the wall, on the pictures of Frederick the Great and the Führer and a herd of sheep grazing between juniper and birches; on the limp flag and the white sheets and pillows on the floor. Kate lay still, listening. Ose, next to her, was breathing with her mouth open, Kriemhild, on her other side, was munching softly in her sleep. Straw rustled as a girl mumbled and turned. Straw pricked Kate's skin. The sheet and blanket were rumpled, and straw had crept inside her pajamas. She sat up and scratched. In the wall opposite were four large luminous squares. Maren had let them raise the black-out curtains and open the windows last night after lights-out to get rid of the dust and the stifling, stale heat.

Kate fell back. The layer of straw made a hard bed, but she did not mind; she was happy. Everything yesterday had worked out well, she thought. Maren had simply asked for the village school across the green and had been handed the key by a taciturn farmer, the mayor of Decherow, who used his empty left sleeve to wipe his neck. The school was a low thatched-roof building, walled in, with brick floors, three classrooms, a hall, one tiny teachers' lounge with couch, desk, and bookshelf, a cinder-covered yard with a rickety picnic table, a flagpole, and an outhouse.

"What is that?" Ose had asked innocently, and Kriemhild had explained it to her with squeals of laughter.

"Can't you tell by the smell?"

"And where do we wash and bathe?" Ose had still looked rather dubious.

"There's the trough and the pump on the green." More laughter.

"With the whole village watching?" With a wild shriek Ose had rushed at the bunch of local kids and their dogs, and together they had all chased them out of the compound.

It had been fun to turn the school into their own hostel. One classroom was cleared for sleeping. Wheezing and sneezing in the clouds of dust, they had dragged bales of straw inside to spread on the grimy floor—two rows with a central aisle. Maren had insisted on almost too much neatness, with sheets and blankets and pillows and packs and other belongings in precise order, and she had not cared for Kate's joking about the jade-green blanket among the mud-brown. She had ordered Trudy into the most distant corner, behind the teachers' desk, which had been too heavy to move.

The second classroom had been arranged for meetings and meals, with a large center table, their own flag, a map of Europe with the various theaters of war marked with colored pins, and a large portrait of Adolf Hitler from the teachers' room. All the while the village kids had hung around outside, trying to peek through holes and scratches in the white paint that blinded the windows.

Sylvia had gone off and returned with a bedroll and cart

full of food—sandwiches, apples, milk—and a mute older woman in scarf and dark dress and rough wooden clogs.

"I put up the kichen at the farm next door. This is Olga—she'll work for us," Sylvia had declared, and with a quick succession of orders had sent the woman running. "You kids want to eat outside?"

"Hurrah, hurrah!"

Toward the end of a noisy supper Sylvia had placed a finger on her lips and pointed to the wall. They all had watched a visored cap appear. "The village idiot," someone had whispered, and they had applauded loudly when Sylvia had knocked the cap down by throwing one of the apples fast and accurately. Sigrid had retrieved the hat and was going to wear it when Brunhild had wrestled it away from her and flung it back over the wall. It was only after the evening flag ceremony and the final song that Maren had told Sylvia that she could not have the teachers' lounge for herself.

"We are one group, comrades," Maren had said, sticking her chin out, looking past Sylvia, and fingering the red-and-white rope across her chest. "No extras, no special treatment. We are here together."

Sylvia had smiled.

Kate thought of her sister among the sleeping girls, under the second window to her left. Sylvia would not remain long in the same room with them, not after her performance last night.

"Last spring, when I flew up to Norway near the polar circle, we slept on dry moss." Her voice had sung out. "That's all that grows up there—moss and scraggly pines and bitter red berries."

"You do get around, don't you?" Marianne had remarked into the respectful silence. "How come?"

"Uncle Hermann arranged it. It's beautiful up there." Sylvia had sounded as casual as if she'd been talking about a Sunday afternoon family outing, a trip to the park, a hike around a lake. Norway was enemy territory and had been occupied by the German Army since 1940. Sylvia had gone on to tell them about smoked reindeer hams, and the green stuff inside their stomachs, and how the Eskimo loved it, and about a raid in the midnight sun.

"I'll show you my scar tomorrow."

Nobody had asked about Uncle Hermann. Kate was convinced Sylvia would have told them with truthful glee that she meant Field Marshal Hermann Göring, Vice Chancellor of Germany and an old air force buddy of their father's from World War I. Kate, too, called him uncle and could conjure up his ringed, perfumed hand patting her cheek, though there was no need to talk about it here. Kate liked secrets, and she also preferred to remain in the background.

She had enjoyed listening to Sylvia in the dark, feeling strong and protected with nobody knowing about their bond. What luck to be in the same camp as her sister!

"Katie, please, you'll get my trunk today, won't you? There's a bus at eleven-thirty." Sylvia shook her awake, keeping her voice down, when the sun sparkled behind the frosted glass. Someone had already closed the windows. "Lend me your comb and toothbrush."

Kate dug them out of her pack. Brunhild, wrapped mummylike, lay motionless; the other twin was now brushing Sylvia's hair, flaunting a golden brush, while Inga was folding her blanket. Maren's corner was shipshape. Then she and Frokke and Sigrid tiptoed into the room and started to play their recorders. They were out of tune, Sigrid surprisingly more skillful than the others, who doggedly trailed a note or two behind. Kate liked their playing. She liked it better than Belinda's pulling the covers off to get her out of bed. So she joined into the song. "When the early dew is falling tra-la-la-la-la-la-la . . .''

The awkward trunk! Kate could understand that Sylvia wasn't free just before mealtime to slip off to Gatow. Kate would have to do it. For a moment she thought of asking one of the twins, since they already knew about the trunk. But that would mean siding with them. And she'd much rather befriend Ose or Inga or Marianne, who'd soon be leading others in their own right, while the twins were fun but too peculiar. She could manage alone.

Laughing and giggling and chatting with one another, the girls dressed, washed superficially at the trough, dashed after two early snot-nosed spectators and a flock of chickens and ducks, straightened their quarters, and assembled for roll call under the flag.

Breakfast came—the ordeal Kate expected it to be. There was the dreary Olga serving soup—sweetened, lukewarm boiled milk thickened with lumps of flour. At home Kate would have balked and left the table hungry. Warm milk made her want to vomit, and the thought of its skin sticking to the roof of her mouth sent shivers down her back. Here she forced down a couple of spoonfuls. Let her stomach revolt! Kate did not want to be weak. Everybody liked milk, hot chocolate, puddings, custards, so it should not be difficult to swallow them. It was only a question of being strong-willed enough, as she had been told time and again. Today she was going to win. She finished her soup.

"Seconds!" demanded the girls.

Olga rounded the table, refilling bowls and dumping another ladle into Kate's before she could stop her. Kate groaned inwardly.

"I'll eat it." Sylvia reached for the bowl. "I'm always hungry."

She made a great show of gulping down the soup, and everybody laughed.

After breakfast Maren called for order.

"A Hitler Youth camp is war service," she said, her large teeth biting into the words. "We are here to do our duty. And I want us to be the best group in the district, better than the kids at the hostel."

The girls cheered.

She went on to talk about their job of gathering plants for medicinal use as drugs, ointments, lotions, compresses, and for brewing teas. Local herbs were needed as substitutes for substances that had been imported before the war. This was their contribution to the war effort.

It was nothing new. For the past two summers students had been required to collect various plants and deliver them at their schools. There were quotas: two pounds of elderberry blossoms, one pound of yarrow leaves, half a pound of chamomile, three ounces of the white flowers of the dead nettle, and so on.

"You know, Kate, I've no idea what to look for!" Sylvia had exclaimed last summer. "You don't want me to poison the teas, do you?" She had paid Kate handsomely to collect her required amount.

Kate did know plants. Biology was her favorite subject,

and she was herb warden in her class. That was why she had opted for this camp instead of helping on a farm or choosing other work. And she had assumed that her comrades felt the way she did. But Kriemhild, for example, couldn't tell peas from beans, unless they were on her plate, she had said.

"We'll divide the area and explore in three groups." Maren sketched a rough map of Decherow on the blackboard—the triangle of the green, the main road from Gatow to Bollhagen coming from the south and cutting through the center of the village eastward, a third road leading west-northwest into the thick chalk lines of the state forest, the hostel, and a meandering line into the right-hand corner.

"The Deche. It isn't much of a river, but there's a swimming hole."

"The afternoon treat," Sylvia said, beaming.

In the sections, separated by the roads, Maren printed her own name, Frokke's, and Marianne's—the leaders—and counted out the girls. "The state forest is strictly off limits. And stay within a circle of three miles!" she warned. "We want to know what and how much is growing where." Then she copied the names of different plants from a list.

"You know what to look for?"

Frokke, Marianne, Inga, and Sigrid nodded, and in her own group Kate and Ose did too.

"Dismissed."

As Kate went to pick up her gear, her shoulder bag and the guide to Central European wild flowers, she saw that Sylvia's bedding was gone.

The girls parted on the green, each group with a couple of village kids pursuing them. Kate's group went last, with

41◇

Maren leading, and as they turned into the Bollhagen road, Kate thought she saw the harelipped boy glide out of the shelter behind the war memorial. He was their only hanger-on. She'd have to evade him and the group, Kate thought, when she stole away to the station. It was the wrong way to start camp, but she could not let her sister down. Although shouldn't she feel more loyal to the group? It was troubling.

The Bollhagen road, treeless now, hemmed in by fields of beets and potatoes, sloped uphill. Walking at a brisk pace, they reached the summit. A closed army truck rumbled past, and Kate watched its trail of dust down into Decherow and along the state forest road. Ahead, the road curved around smaller fields and meadows, skirted hedges, rounded thickets and clumps of trees and bushes. The sky was very blue.

"We'll work our way back to the Gatow road in a slow arc," Maren instructed them. "Keep your eyes open."

She led them into a deeply rutted lane. Kate noted tansy, yarrow, broad-leaved plantain at the wayside, a yellow-green cushion of useless toadflax, shepherd's purse, bluebells. There was a belt of stinging nettles and raspberry canes surrounding the thicket.

Maren told them to fan out and meet under an oak tree, exposed and huge and an hour's walk away. That was when Kate began her run for Gatow. First she kept low, moved slowly, stealthily; then she ran openly, traversed pastures, crossed fields, galloped along tracks. She was going to make up for deserting her group, she promised herself. And make up she did by discovering a tract of chamomile, especially valued, at least ten pounds of white and yellow blossoms still on the stem. Once she saw the harelipped boy and raised her fist at him. Why couldn't he spy on Maren and the others?

She was right on time at the bus stop, breathless, the trunk at her feet, only to find out that the bus ran twice a week. Tomorrow, not today. For a long time she simply sat on the grotesque piece of luggage. Then she remembered the boy. He was certainly as strong as she was.

"Hey, you," she called when she saw him lurking inside the station. "Hey, come here, will you?"

He came.

"Why are you following me?"

"Just curious."

He did look repulsive, the upper lip pulled in a permanent grin, the scar tissue deadly white in his sunburned face. His speech was distorted too. His hair was cut short and bristly. Today he was not wearing his cap. His faded blue shirt was mended, his long pants not long enough, his bare feet in sandals. He carried a tattered bag. She couldn't bring herself to ask him for help, she decided; he was too disgusting.

"Hotel Martinique, Broadway and 32nd Street, New York," he read. "Funny trunk. And you have a pack too—I saw you arrive yesterday."

She glared at him.

"There is no bus," he stated.

"I know," she snapped.

"We could carry it together." He did not seem to feel as ill at ease as she did.

So she set out a second time for Decherow. Kate sang, pushing the words between clenched teeth. Soon her throat was dry, her shoulders ached, her arms and hands became lame. They paused more and more often. They sat on the trunk, legs dangling, watching the road for signs of life. He offered her a handful of pea pods out of his bag. She liked them.

"I'm almost thirteen," she said. "And you?"

"Twelve."

"What's your name?"

"Harry."

Harelipped Harry, she thought.

"Harelipped Harry," he said with his terrible grin.

After another hundred yards Kate opened the trunk, found a lemon cake with raisins, and broke off big chunks for Harry and herself. He stored most of his share inside his bag.

"For my friends," he said.

They sat munching.

"I have a scar on my forehead," said Kate. "It's small, though. My sister and I played blindman's buff, and I walked into a lamppost with my eyes blindfolded."

"Funny guide," he remarked.

"Oh, but it was my fault—she'd warned me."

Kate recalled piloting a blind Sylvia home from school. The next day, when it was her turn to be led, a group of her sister's friends came frolicking along. Rapt, Sylvia was topping one of their jokes, and her "Watch out!" had been slow.

He heard the engine first.

"It's the mayor," said Harry. "He'll give you a ride. See you around."

Seconds later he had vanished. Kate did not call him back.

She would have been embarrassed to have been seen with him.

"Ride?" It was the mayor on a tractor, towing a wagon.

Kate nodded, her mouth still full of cake.

"Get the Ivans off!"

She watched several men drop clumsily down from the open wagon. A young soldier, his rifle slung across his back, lifted her and the trunk onto the wagon. Then the tractor chugged forward, and she was pushed onto a makeshift bench. A second soldier, an elderly man, a rifle in his lap, smiled broadly at her. There were six men walking behind their vehicle in the churned-up dirt. The young soldier kept himself in the shade at the roadside.

"Quick, quick! Keep up!"

The men's faces were filthy, unshaven, dull, coarse, and foreign, their uniforms torn and unkempt, their feet in rags. They were prisoners of war, and they did look inferior, Kate thought.

Abruptly she turned to the elderly soldier. "May I hold your rifle?"

He handed it over. It felt heavy and smooth and smelled of hot grease.

Kate swung it around, aiming high.

"Watch it, kid, it's loaded."

"I could hit that bird up there."

"What would you want to do that for? It's a field lark."

He took the rifle back and aimed at the prisoners.

Sylvia was expecting her on the village green.

"You're great," she said, and called her thanks to the mayor and the guards. "It's all set. I told Maren I sent you on an errand. Olga has kept your lunch, but first we'll take the trunk to my room. What would I have done without you, Katie!''

Sylvia's bed was made up on the couch in the teachers' lounge.

SEVEN

◇ I am in Grandma Hofmann's room.

I trail my hand over the sideboard, across the carvings of leaves and flowers, and sniff my fingers. I like the lemon of her furniture polish better than the overpowering anise. I touch and examine all her treasures. I know them, but I like to handle them. I think most of them are beautiful, but I guess I will change my mind when I grow up.

A dark red Bohemian glass bowl—Grandpa Hofmann brought it from Prague on one of his leaves. Then it was filled with delicate chocolates, I was told.

A picture of their wedding. The only one I know of Grandpa without his uniform, and he does not look like a hero. He looks like Mr. Grimmel, who did his student teaching in life sciences in my grade and worried about his experiments and our answers. Grandma is formidable in laced, dainty white boots.

The red wooden triplane, a replica of the aircraft Grandpa piloted during World War I, his Red Baron days. Nick has put down his claim to inherit it, and so have I.

A photograph of Grandpa in the cockpit, with the Red Baron clasping his hand, and his autograph.

A silver tea and coffee set that distorts my face, just like the wavy mirrors at the fair grounds.

Two Japanese dolls, gifts from Aunt Sylvia's travels.

A pair of baby shoes in pure gold, modeled after Dad's.

A set of glass animals I gave Grandma two Christmases ago.

A bird that Nick carved and painted in third grade.

A silver vase and a silver plaque, commemorating the service with the Red Baron.

I wander over to the wall where the photographs are. There again is the Red Baron among the family pictures. The hero, the flying ace, in a heavy frame.

I sit among the pillows on the sofa. They are much softer than ours—real silk and velvet, embroidered, one even glowing in the dark. I stick my face into them. They smell of lavender soap and again of anise. I get up, take one of the pictures off the wall, and retreat to the sofa.

It's a family group, tinted, and I have often been told when and why and where it was taken. There is Grandpa behind a chair, but I can still see the dark red stripes down the side of his pants, the stripes of a general. Grandma is sitting on the chair holding my dad on her lap. He straddles her knees, caught in mid-wobble. He is held from behind, and Sylvia smiles at him and into the camera. The other Kate is standing a little apart, concentrated, serious. Her hair is parted in the middle and braided. Grandma and her daughters are wearing dresses made out of the same material. I would hate that, and so would Mom.

Grandma and Aunt Sylvia and Bozo come into the room.

"Oh, here you are!" Grandma and Aunt Sylvia cry in unison.

I should not be here uninvited.

Aunt Sylvia takes the picture away from me and looks at

it. She chuckles. "You remember Sven Peter making such a fuss about the poor photographer, Mother? Every time Mr. Beling disappeared under his black cloth, Sven Peter screamed and screamed."

Grandma nods and smiles. "And you played the piano to calm him. Your Aunt Sylvia was such a talented player. Too bad she couldn't keep it up."

"Yes—the war," replies my aunt.

I gave up piano lessons after four months. I was no good at it.

"Those dresses were lovely," gushes Aunt Sylvia. "Such exquisite material. From France, wasn't it?"

"What's that above their heads?" I ask.

Aunt Sylvia's laughter peals through the room. "It's the tip of your grandpa's propeller," she says. "The one thing I'm glad we lost in the war."

I get Grandma's magnifying glass and look at it. It is just a piece of wood, well polished, and I cannot discover any fingerprints. I pore over the faces one after the other.

"You sister has a scar on her forehead," I say.

"Nonsense." Grandma reaches for the picture. "It's a speck of dirt, nothing else."

Aunt Sylvia bends over the glass, goes back to the table, turns on a second lamp. Then she dissolves in merriment.

"Oh, yes, the scar! I remember now. We walked around with our eyes closed. And she bumped into something—a lamppost! Smack! The weird games kids think of!"

Grandma's cheeks quiver.

Aunt Sylvia signals me to leave.

EIGHT

July 4, 1943

Snubbing Sylvia was Maren's downfall. Kate thought that it served her right, because there had been no reason to reject the proposal except that it had come from Sylvia. The girls had loved it. But it was only the beginning of a series of rebuffs.

" 'Duty comes first,' Maren said, and she canceled the swimming," reported Sylvia as they left her room, the trunk safely tucked away. "She's boring."

Kate knew that being boring was a major fault.

"We can swim after work," she said reasonably.

"I'm going right now, but I'll show you where your group is after you've eaten." Sylvia was already carrying her towel and bathing suit.

Lunch was lots of stew and noodles and fruit gelatin, which Kate loved, and a whole pitcher of juice, and Kate felt revived.

They took a footpath between farms, stepping over one of the skinny dogs stretched out asleep. The village was dozing. There was no sound but the buzzing of the flies over the open pit with dung. The garden next to it needed watering. The big leaves of the pumpkins were drooping. They walked past an elderberry bush, stripped of its green, along a hedge of hazelnuts. At a ploughed field Sylvia whirled around and launched a barrage of big lumps of dried earth back into the hedge.

"Yacky dogs," she said.

Kate waited for a howl of pain, and thought of harelipped Harry when it remained quiet. A few minutes later she turned around. Nobody was trailing them.

"You keep on straight," her sister said as the path forked. "I'll go left. Sure you don't want to swim? We'll have lots of fun, and I can invent another excuse."

"We shouldn't stick together," Kate reminded her. "Besides, you know I like collecting, and I want to make up for the morning."

Sylvia laughed. "Good old dependable Kate. Maybe I should take you as a model."

"Oh, no. It wouldn't be right for you."

Kate found the group spread around a clump of bushes and low trees, uneven terrain, where the farmers had cast rocks and rusted, broken-down farm implements. Raspberry bushes grew between stinging nettles and briers. Kate reported to Maren, whose face and arms were dotted with hives. Maren said something about next time Kate should speak to her first, about leaving the group, and of course she was right.

"How's the big city?" asked Kriemhild. "Gatow! How exciting! Gosh, these mosquitoes are fierce." Dancing around in her ridiculous pumps, she slapped her arms, legs, face.

But she was the only one who complained, though Frokke's left eye was swollen shut, Trudy had been stung on the nose, and Ose's cheek was scratched bloody.

Kate enjoyed gathering the leaves. Insects did not bother her, and she worked fast. When Maren blew her whistle for them to stop, Kate's bag was as tightly filled as the others'. All their legs were crisscrossed with red streaks. They all itched, and they were weary.

They had bread and tea for supper. Sylvia bounced around the table, fresh and cool in a sleeveless blouse.

"Is that the scar you got in Norway?" Marianne asked her, and everyone stopped eating and stared at the whitish line on Sylvia's upper arm.

"Yeah . . . the wound was five inches long and an inch deep and needed fourteen stitches. There was no anesthesia. It was shrapnel that did it. I keep it as a souvenir on my desk at home."

Kate had heard other versions: the grazing bullet of a Polish partisan, the barbed wire of the Maginot Line, the branch of a tree while parachuting down. Sylvia was such an accomplished liar!

"Did you cry?" Kate asked. Now all eyes turned and were fixed on Kate coldly.

"I mean, it must have hurt," she stammered, thinking of Sylvia's deafening screams as the vines at the window gave and she crashed to the bottom.

"A German girl does not cry." Sylvia spoke lightly, yet left no doubt. Then she turned to all the girls. "How about a game of volley ball?"

"Sounds great."

"Yes, let's play!"

"You'll be team captain, won't you?"

One girl was shouting louder than the other.

"Attention!" Maren's voice hacked through the din. They

leaped up, stood frozen, arms pressed to their sides.

"I think we need more discipline," Maren said pointedly. "Fall in for roll call outside in three minutes sharp. In uniform."

She walked out, and the girls scrambled for the door. Kate noticed her sister smile and shrug and tell Olga to clear the table.

And Sylvia had fruit juice ready for them when Maren finally let them go after inspection and prolonged drilling—cool delicious juice, as much as they could drink.

"Last year at my camp we raided another camp, paid them a surprise visit during the night. That was a lot of fun." Again all eyes were on Sylvia, and a sigh of pleasure went through the room.

"I am camp leader," Maren broke in, and Kate thought she must be standing on a book or a brick; she seemed so much taller. "I think it would be better if you conferred with me before . . . I have other plans for the group tonight. We worked hard and we need sleep."

"No need to pull rank! Who said anything about tonight?" Sylvia was mocking her. "I was only telling a story. Good night and Heil Hitler."

Most of the girls looked after her with regret, thought Kate. A raid would have been fun.

The dream began harmlessly enough. Strapped into her buggy, Kate was being pushed along a bumpy road. She was wriggling, trying to squirm out of her covers. She longed to catch one of the exploding stars, the shiny bright fragments of fireworks raining down. Then panic swept her as her arms were pinned to her sides. She was bigger now; she knew she had to get up and put on her sweat suit and run to the cellar, but she could not move. Tracer lights flashed across the sky; a Christmas tree lit up, bathing the room in phosphorous white; the beams of searchlights fingered through the darkness. It was an air raid, and she had not heard the wail of the siren, but she had to get up!

Something weighed her down; her arms were straitjacketed into the blanket. Kate craned her head to escape the blinding light. Then the explosion caught hold of her, battered her, and in the end flung her on the landing between the rubber plant and the aspidistra, among pails with sand and water. Again immobile, squeezed under the banister, she heard the sirens howl. There were flames on the attic stairs, and there was Sylvia fighting the fire with the wet mop. Smack, smack, she was hitting Kate right in the face. Once, twice, again and again.

"No! Stop it! Stop it!" Kate bellowed, struggling up.

The wetness was real enough; so were the noise and the lights. Someone was sitting on her, whipping her face with a wet rag. She smelled the foul odor of dishwater. Flashlights flickered over the ceiling, the walls, the people.

The Youth Hostel kids! An ambush! The kids from the Youth Hostel had stolen a march on them. They were being raided.

"Oohoohoohoohoohoohoo!" The attackers were swarming through the windows, white sheets flapping.

"Oohoohoohoohoohoohoo!" They swung their soggy wet towels, face cloths, dishrags, mops.

"The enemy!" Kate, wide-awake, hurled herself into the fight. She snatched a towel from one of the raiders and twirled it around, slapping blindly. Someone grabbed it away from her. She tackled a sheeted figure, and together they rolled in the straw. A flashlight gleamed over the other's face.

"Inga! I'm sorry." Feeling sheepish, Kate let her go.

She was punched from behind and plunged into a group of kids. A sneaker kicked her, and she tore it off, whacked heads and backs and threw the sneaker out of the window. She thought she saw Frokke's small eyes and heard Kriemhild's sneering.

"Cowards! Low, sneaking cretins! Master race, my foot! You bastards!"

Kate was toppled, and she and the other kid were wrestling on the floor, in and out of the straw. It was a boy, and Kate was as strong as he. No one would have won if he had not gotten tangled in his sheet. Soon she had swaddled him from head to foot. Clutching her catch, she lay close to him, laughing.

"Blackout curtains! Damned kids! Want to bring the bombs down on us? Lights out!"

Kate was sure it was Sylvia, her voice disguised, rough. How clever of her! Instantly the flashlights died and the fighting stopped. A signal sounded softly, and the kids from the hostel slunk to the windows, glided over the sills, and vanished on the green.

"We won!" cried Sylvia in her normal voice. "That was simply great! Wonderful!"

She dashed to close the curtains and switched on the light. The room was a mess. Blankets, sheets, pillows jumbled together, packs overturned, clothing thrown around, and straw covering everything. All the girls spoke at once. Only Maren was silent, leaning against the wall under the picture of the Führer, gaping at the chaos. Sylvia was prancing around the room. It was weird, Kate thought, how her sister had turned a sure defeat into a glorious victory.

"I've got a prisoner." Kate had to say it twice before anyone paid attention. "What am I going to do with my prisoner?"

"Prisoner?" Kate and her bundle were surrounded. The girls stared down, poked with their feet. The bundle remained mute and stiff.

"A prisoner! Who captured him? Maren? No? Kate? That's wonderful!" Sylvia gushed, taking over. "We'll throw him outside, but first let's have a look at the hero." She unwrapped his head, while waves of giggles swept through the room. The boy's bulging light eyes glared at them. There was a trace of dark hair growing on his upper lip.

"Shame on you! Taken prisoner by a girl!" Sylvia made fun of him. "What's your name?"

The boy was biting his lip.

"Name and rank," barked Ose and Marianne.

"How many in your unit?" prodded Frokke.

The prisoner closed his eyes.

"Gosh, I'm tired. Let's get some sleep soon, or I'll want a mid-morning nap." Kriemhild and her twin yawned.

Then Sylvia ordered them to carry the boy outside. The village green was deserted, and the war memorial shone metallic in the moonlight.

"Let's sacrifice him to the gods of war," Sylvia whispered dramatically.

So, four on each side, the girls transported their bundle across to the memorial, while the others escorted them. Under Sylvia's direction they draped him like an offering between the dying soldiers under the avenging angel. Then they held hands and danced around the monument.

"Like the Rhine maidens," remarked Kriemhild. "Rhine maidens in pajamas."

Only Sylvia looked beautiful in her long nightgown, with the moonlight gleaming in her hair, thought Kate. Now Sylvia stepped out of the circle to place the wreath against the prisoner.

"He will die so that Germany lives," she quoted in a vibrant voice.

One dog barked and then another and another.

It was Sylvia and not Maren who gave the hushed command to retreat and go back to bed.

"Yacky dogs," she said. "Now they'll never stop. We'd better break it up. Group dismissed!" The girls followed her into the school, Maren and Frokke the last ones.

"Of course you'll have to act tomorrow! Raid the hostel," Sylvia told them before she shut the door to her room. "That's the only honorable response. Otherwise they'll think you're cowards. Well, good night again, and Heil Hitler."

On her bed of rumpled straw Kate thought that Maren had acted as if she had been demoted. Not like the seventh grader, Karla, who had been found to be a thief and had been stripped of her insignia on the parade ground on April twentieth, Hitler's birthday. The entire group had been lined up for flag ceremony. Stealing was contemptible, an act against the community, and Kate would never serve under someone like Karla.

No, Maren had acted more like Dr. Witkowsky, the school principal, who two years ago had addressed all school assemblies, but who seemed to have been replaced by the erect

Dr. Ott. Now every student knew that "go and see the principal" meant a visit to Dr. Ott's office. Dr. Witkowsky still held the title, but it was no longer comfortable to meet him in the hallways or on the stairs. And it would be uncomfortable to face Maren tomorrow. But wasn't it the right of the strong to lead?

Maren was very busy issuing orders the next morning and setting up the day's program, as if she had arranged it all in her mind during the night. Camp chores, plant collecting, drill, instruction, games. And the counterattack at night.

Kate was detailed to clean up the dormitory.

"Shipshape, you understand, shipshape!" Maren said. She was too shrill.

NINE

◇ On Monday Aunt Sylvia comes to pick me up after school. She is waiting under a large polka-dotted umbrella, with Bozo on a leash. I had hoped the steady cool drizzle would keep her away. She waves excessively as I come out of the east gate with my friends.

"I got your mom's Rabbit, Kate." Her voice rings across the yard. "Let's see how many of you we can squeeze inside."

It's an old joke; nevertheless we dash for the car. We are nine people, three up front and six in the back, plus Bozo. The windows steam up, and Bozo wiggles to lick them clean.

"We didn't break the world record, but with my driver's license expired I've got to be careful," declares Aunt Sylvia, and my friends laugh. "You don't have to go home right away, do you?"

"Oh, no, oh, no, oh, no!" Bozo howls along with all of us.

Last year we made Aunt Sylvia honorary member of our secret society. Last year we took her blindfolded to our headquarters in Werner's backyard, let her climb the fence, crawl under the privet hedge, circle the carport three times, and touch a series of wet, slimy objects. We brewed tea from nettles for her in our underground warren and basked in pleasure as she cried out in amazement at our setup—the rugs, the furniture, the pictures.

This year the secret society is disbanding. We did not fix the warren after the March earth slide; Werner's younger brother inherited it. We have other interests now. There is no need to expel Aunt Sylvia.

"What about bowling?" my aunt asks, and we cheer. Trust her to propose just the right treat for a rainy afternoon, grown-up and rare enough, irresistible.

Today she takes care not to win.

"Good shot," she calls encouragingly.

"Great job!" She slaps backs. My friends love her and envy me. I pat Bozo.

She takes off her cardigan, weighs the bowling ball in her hand, launches it down the center of the lane. It knocks down six pins, and she leaps up, clapping. My friends see the scar on her upper arm and ask about it.

"A machete," she says. "Going up Machu Picchu in South America, I was caught in a train robbery. They didn't expect me to fight back, but I would never let them take me prisoner."

She speaks casually, and I can see that my friends think she's great.

She orders Cokes and hamburgers and ham sandwiches and ice cream and fruit tarts and a large beer for herself. Everybody is allowed to take a swig. Bozo's nose is white with foam.

"You must tell me all about your class trip. Camping, wasn't it?" she says, and in the same breath goes on. "I did a lot of camping in California with my troop. I used to be a Girl Scout leader.''

Aunt Sylvia swings into her Allison Tenant stories, which I love. Allison Tenant, another Scout leader, frail, absent-minded, impractical. I see Allison Tenant leading a troop of girls into the Mojave Desert, canteen leaking. I watch her poring over the mail with a magnifying glass, hunting for reusable stamps; a penny saved is a penny earned. I have heard about how Allison, at the campfire, telling about the hangman's tree, trembles so much that the girls have to comfort her.

"A funny old bird," muses Aunt Sylvia. "Not at all what the scout law asks for. 'Quick as a greyhound, tough as leather, and hard as steel'—isn't that it?''

" 'A scout is trustworthy, loyal, helpful, friendly, courteous, kind, obedient, cheerful, thrifty, brave, clean, reverent,' '' I recite, correcting her.

"And long-winded!" adds Aunt Sylvia. My friends chuckle.

"I'm sure you're right, Katie dear.'' She smiles at me. Again I feel petty.

"We staged a night raid on our camping trip,'' says my friend Werner.

"How marvelous! Tell me all about it.''

Werner talks and we all listen.

It had been my idea, modeled after the diary—wet towels and white sheets in the dead of night. We did not lose anybody. We roused the police, and they grumbled and laughed.

There was no honor involved.

TEN

🦋 *July 5, 1943*

In a way even the enemy—the British and the Americans—were siding against Maren, Kate thought idly. And Kriemhild had been granted her wish. She would be rolled up, napping, somewhere nearby in the shade.

Maren had marched the group along the state forest road and then left along a ridge. Just when they had reached their goal—a field lying fallow with a sprinkling of chamomile conspicuous among the weeds—the air alarm had sounded. The first wail had come from beyond Gatow. It had traveled to other villages, and finally Decherow was warning urgently. Maren had told the girls to scatter and seek shelter. "Everybody stay put till the all-clear. Is that understood?"

Kate had sprinted toward the edge of the forest, slightly uphill, and now she was sitting on a pillow of moss, overlooking the countryside. She was munching sweet young carrots. Harelipped Harry, sitting on a stump, was munching too. They were his carrots, stolen out of the mayor's garden, he said, but Kate did not believe him. She thought he was boasting. He could not eat with his mouth closed.

"I watched you come running," he said. "You always run for cover?"

"You always spy on people?"

"Yes." He did not seem to resent her question.

"It's an order to seek cover. Because of strafing." Kate scanned the sky. Recently she had seen a newsreel of American aircraft machine-gunning civilians.

"*They* don't hide." Harry pointed to a row of distant figures hoeing in the middle of an endless field.

"You should report them to the air warden. It's dangerous for them," she said severely.

"But the warden knows it." Harry grinned lopsidedly. "They're working his field. They're the mayor's prisoners, and I guess he must be air warden."

"Well, that's different. They wouldn't be shot at by their own side."

"And how could you tell from up there?" His voice was teasing.

"Signals," Kate replied curtly. "All you need is a mirror." Then she thought that the prisoners behind the open cart yesterday had not looked as if they owned a mirror. They had looked as if they possessed nothing.

"We'll watch them." Arms folded around her knees, Kate let her eyes wander between sky and field. The sky was pale blue near the horizon and very blue and empty toward the center. The prisoners did not interrupt their hurried rhythm of hoeing.

Then she heard the planes coming. The faint and faraway humming grew into a steady drone. The planes flew in formation, silver specks arranged high up in neat order. Kate was dazzled. It was the first time she had seen so many of them. At home she would be crammed in a shelter, behind walls, deep below the ground. Only once her father had shown her an enemy bomber, caught at night in the beams of two searchlights.

She counted two hundred and twenty planes.

"Where do you think they're going?"

"Berlin, of course."

A hoe glinted in the sun. Was it a signal?

"Three hundred and forty." Kate was cold with anger. They were flying up there as if the sky belonged to them! Why didn't the fighter planes blow up their formation? Why didn't she see the white puffs of the antiaircraft shells exploding? In newsreels the camera always followed the dark smoky trail of an enemy plane and watched it tumble from the sky.

"What's it like—a bombing raid?" Harry was staring into the sky.

"It makes me want to shoot them down, every single one of them!" Kate replied.

Then the planes were gone and the drone faded and died. For a long time everything was quiet. The prisoners were still working.

"Do you want me to show you a secret?" the boy asked, pulling his cap far down over his face.

"No, thanks," Kate said. What kind of secret could he have! Besides, she had spent enough time with him. And she had not chosen his company. But she went on to explain that her group was expecting her. As the all-clear blew, she trotted off without looking back at him.

There was no need for Maren to tell the group to make up for the time lost. The girls scurried across the field, swooping down on the pungent flowers to fill their bags.

And it was easy, Kate observed. There was no other white and yellow blossom. Even Kriemhild, flushed with sleep, wouldn't make mistakes, or the bumbling Trudy. When they trudged back and emptied their harvest in the school attic, Maren announced proudly that they had topped their quota.

"So we're free to play a game after lunch," she said, and she proposed an arrow hunt. "It's a great way to check out the terrain."

There was a hum of excitement.

"It's a wonderful game! I'll join you." Sylvia had popped into the attic.

"Don't you have other responsibilities?" Maren asked sourly.

"Oh, Olga can do without me."

"Sure, you can play." Maren gave in. "You know the rules, don't you?"

There was nobody who knew the rules better than Sylvia, Kate thought. Back in Berlin she was famous for this game. Kate remembered the hours spent hiding in some strange garage or attic or backyard, waiting in agreeable terror to be found and pounced upon either by the owner or the team of hunters. Hiding in Herder's restroom and pretending to be one of the customers had been the worst.

"Sylvia and I will be team captains," Maren announced.

"I'm for Maren!"

"Take me, take me, Sylvia!"

"Let's eat first. Aren't you starving?"

Later, out on the green, the girls crowded around their captains. They all longed to be among the first to be selected for the two teams—the hunters and the hiders. Alternately Maren and Sylvia picked their teammates, while the village kids and their dogs watched, with Harry, as usual, standing apart.

And yet he had talked about saving the cake for his friends, Kate remembered.

"Frokke." Frokke looked smug. She had been chosen.

"Marianne." Marianne suppressed a grin.

So it went. All the girls Kate liked best, even Kriemhild, were already on Sylvia's team, and she wished her sister would finally call her name. Sylvia really went too far in pretending to have nothing to do with her. She must know how disappointed Kate would be if she got stuck in Maren's faction.

"Trudy!" Trudy glowed and joined Sylvia's side.

Maren chose Kate and also asked for the hunter's part in the game. Kate felt sorry for herself and almost sorry for Maren. Now defeat for her team was inevitable. In Sylvia's schemes the hunters always lost. But shouldn't the best one win?

"Wouldn't you kids like to play?" Sylvia turned to their spectators.

"You mean it?" Their mouths dropped open. Harry moved closer.

"All right, everybody?" Sylvia addressed both teams.

The girls and Maren nodded.

"But morons and dogs are out," Sylvia said, and there was laughter.

Kate wondered if Harry expected her to stand up for him. She was slow in walking over to where he stood beyond her comrades. Just then Sylvia assigned Harry to Maren's team. To spite her, Kate thought.

The game began. Maren and her team of hunters went

inside for a twenty-minute wait to give the hiders a lead. The hiders would draw an arrow in the dirt of the green, clearly visible, pointed, and another arrow thirty yards away, and so on—a trail of arrows. The trail would end two hours later with a huge swastika, the final mark. The hiders themselves would be hiding near it.

"And our team tracks the arrows," Kate told Harry. "Drawing arrows—that's an art. You don't write them with chalk on a tree or a wall. They're not exactly road signs. You camouflage them, build them out of twigs and pebbles, blend them with the stuff around them, put them high or low. If we find the other team in time, we win."

They were milling around the yard, waiting for Maren's signal. Harry had offered Kate a handful of sunflower seeds, and she admired the way he shelled them rapidly, using his teeth and tongue. She needed four fingers to get at the seed.

At last Maren released them. "Twenty minutes, on the dot."

The first arrow on the green was large and carelessly edged into the ground, directing them to the Bollhagen road. So they set out, Maren and Frokke and their eight teammates and four of the village kids. The dogs were kicked back and didn't seem to mind.

Kate and Harry made up the rear. Kate knew most of Sylvia's tricks and she did not feel like watching Maren fall for them. And fall she would—plain, correct, dull Maren. Instead Kate talked to Harry about Sylvia's tactics. "There are straightforward arrow hunts and others with twists," she said as they trudged over rough ground parallel to the main road. "And we'll be back on the Bollhagen road with time lost."

"I bet they sent one of their fast kids to mark the half circle while the rest took it easy on the main road," observed Harry.

"How did you guess?" Kate looked at him, startled. He was right, as she well knew.

"How did *you* guess?" He gave his own answer. "You and the other girl, Sylvia, are both from Berlin. You must have been on the same team before."

He wasn't stupid, Kate thought; she'd have to be careful.

Twice their entire team filed around a clump of trees; here the arrows were stripped raspberry canes woven into the underbrush. Harry and Kate discovered them at the same time, long before Maren or Frokke did.

"They must have backtracked," he reasoned when no more arrows could be spotted ahead and Maren asked them to spread out. Kate heard him grunt contentedly when he sighted the arrow. Frokke stumbled across it by chance.

Later Sylvia's hiders did a pattern of back and forth, back and forth, along the furrows of a field of potatoes, and Kate and Harry followed it, amused. By now Maren was even more shrill with frustration.

Soon they must reach the spot where Sylvia and her team crossed their own tracks, Kate thought. Sylvia nearly always did a loop, and she loved to watch the other team head along a lengthy and by now futile route.

Kate looked around for a likely place to hide—a barn, a thicket, a hillock. "What a lot of tansy!" she said. "We should pick it tomorrow."

Up on the rim of an abandoned sandpit flared the yellow flowering tansy in thick tufts. The pit was small and almost overgrown except for a vertical strip of sand directly below the overhanging layer of earth and tangled roots. As Kate and Harry stared up, a lump of earth broke off and rolled down, leaving a faint print in the sand. The tansies did not stir. There was one guffaw, quickly smothered.

Kate was convinced the hiders were crouched behind the dense vegetation. She imagined them gloating, their hands pressed over their mouths. Very slowly she went after her own team.

"I saw her—I saw Sylvia and her team," sputtered Harry. "They're in back of us. Now they'll just stroll into the village and we'll find the big swastika right on the green. Can they do it? I don't think it's fair."

"It's within the rules." Kate was gruff. "Maren never had a chance. She's no match for Sylvia."

"Aren't you going to tell your captain?"

Suddenly Kate no longer wanted to be part of the game. "No," she said. "I quit. Show me your secret."

Harry must have sensed her weariness because he waved her abruptly into the stalks of corn to their left and they crouched away from the two factions. When Kate straightened up to glance around, she saw that they had traveled over a knoll, and a deserted pasture sloped down to the edge of a forest. They climbed a fence, sprinted across grass, climbed a second fence, and dived into the brush.

Kate followed Harry over a carpet of leaves. "Is this the state forest?"

"Yeah."

"I thought it was closed off."

"It is," Harry said. "There are notices all around it: 'Do not enter! Unauthorized persons will be shot without warning.' It does keep people away."

"That's why you like it." She could understand him. His awful grin crossed his face.

They walked among the silver branches of beeches and the dark ones of pines. Now they came to a brook, zigzaging, murmuring, alive. Leaping from bank to bank, balancing on boulders, trying out fragile bridges of dead wood and treacherous leaves, Harry led Kate upstream. He seemed to know which rock was level, which slippery, which patch of ground soggy. He must come here often, Kate realized.

"Why is it off limits?" she asked, curious.

"There's a prisoner-of-war camp—Russians mainly, I think." He was craning his neck. "Do you hear the cuckoo?"

"Cuckoo, cuckoo, tell me how many years I'm going to live," Kate called softly, ready to count the bird's answers, but he must have been disturbed. There were no more cuckoos.

The brook became narrower, the banks steeper, as if part of a miniature gorge, and at its end Harry beckoned her into a hollow.

"This is Glashagen Spring," he said. "It's mine."

It was a spacious hollow, with walls rising all around for twenty or thirty yards, and the canopy of trees shutting out the sky. There were pools of water and plants everywhere, so that the light, filtered through leaves, filled the hollow with a magic green. Like Grandpa's aquarium, Kate thought—a dream tank.

At the far end stood a temple, like the ones Kate had seen depicted in history books and in the prints on the stairs back home—two pillars holding a triangular portico, broad steps, a balustrade, all in white marble. Bushes and trees hugged the small building.

"It's mine," Harry repeated, and Kate did not question it. It was his because he had claimed it when nobody else had.

"It used to be a pumping station for the big estate," he explained. "I try to keep it up. It's hard to get paint and everything. Want some tea?"

Kate nodded, and they threaded their way around the connected pools toward the temple. It was not real marble, Kate saw. It was constructed of wood, and its white paint was peeling off except for a few recently slapped-on patches. Grass pushed between the floorboards, and moss cushioned the steps. Kate sat down in a nest of twigs and dry leaves. Harry slipped behind the building and came back with a smoke-black pot, two mugs, and an armful of kindling.

"Won't the smoke betray us?"

He shook his head. "It gets thinned out."

Kate watched him build the fire in the fieldstone fireplace. He filled the pot from the first pool. He displayed his dried teas.

"What do you want—red raspberry, black raspberry, nettle, mint, dandelion, wild fennel?"

"Mint with black raspberry."

He brewed it in the mugs. The smoke curled upward and dispersed under the ceiling of branches and leaves. It was as safe as he had said. The tea tasted fine. He even provided spoons and sugar. He must have a whole arsenal somewhere in the back, thought Kate, though she wouldn't ask to see it. Harry had already let her into a fantastic secret.

"We danced on the green last night."

"Yeah, I saw you."

"You're always watching," she teased, and went on to tell him about the raid, her prisoner rolled in his own sheet and helpless, and of Sylvia's idea to celebrate their victory.

"Sylvia drove the hostel kids away," Kate said.

"Sylvia!" Harry laughed. "All she did was imitate the mayor's voice."

Kate flared up. "And what did *you* do? Snoop and pry!"

"Forget it and have some more tea," he said peaceably. He took her mug.

"The same mixture? I have to tell you I let the boy go. I don't like prisoners."

They sat and drank their tea and watched the fire die. There were insects on the pool's surface and frogs in the water. Harry cleared everything away; then they raced each other downstream.

ELEVEN

◇　It's Monday night. It still rains, and I hear the drops on the patio. I think of the sunflowers heavy with moisture. Tonight, I am sure, they'll tip over—their roots will no longer hold them up.

"There's nothing on television." Grandma Hofmann closes the TV guide firmly. "I don't understand why they keep raking up the past." She sounds mournful.

"We'll play Monopoly instead," says my aunt. "Isn't it wonderful, the whole family playing together?"

"But it's a school night . . ." Mom begins, then subsides. Dad must have nudged her. With Aunt Sylvia present they both give in.

Nick gets the board. It is an American board, one my aunt brought us years ago. Grandma Hofmann surveys it. Aunt Sylvia loves hotels, just as in real life she sends postcards from the Ritz or the Grand this or that. She is never satisfied with a house or two in Monopoly and gets rid of railroads and industrial property.

Nick buys the waterworks, the railroads, where rents are moderate and the investment is low, and with cautious moves he manages to hang on till the end of the game.

Mom plays along to please us, and she holds the bank

because we all trust her. *She* will not arrange secret loans under the table. Dad practices all year to beat his sister.

"But sisters have a way of punishing you if you succeed," he says. How would he know? He never wins.

Dad says I'm romantic because I love St. Charles Place and the cheap and worthless purple block. But I don't care. I love the names, and I go for colors. Anyway, I am always hoping Chance will rescue me.

Aunt Sylvia has a new system each year. "It's surefire," she says. And it is, for her.

Mom hands out the tokens. Grandma gets the tiny silver biplane Nick and I both contend for. To my brother goes the locomotive, to Dad the ivory elephant, to me the frog. Long ago I declared it my favorite. Now I have to stay with it. The family does not allow change. Mom keeps the Eiffel Tower, and Aunt Sylvia takes out a golden nugget.

"It's real," she says.

Right away Aunt Sylvia is sent by Chance to Boardwalk, and she is clapping her hands, crying how wonderful, while Mom sits in Jail. I am doing all right, picking up some of the property I like best. Then I have a streak of bad luck, leaping from Community Chest to Jail to Free Parking, but Nick buys Park Place. He is tenacious and will cling to it, living off his railroads. Aunt Sylvia's prospects go down.

After the auction Grandma looks surprisingly strong. She owns the red and yellow block with only Atlantic Avenue missing, and she barters it from Dad. Aunt Sylvia and Nick conspire to make me pay an enormous sum for Tennessee Avenue. Mom will be out quickly with only the light blue block. Aunt Sylvia's real estate is scattered, so she can't build right away. Grandma selects three houses for her properties. I think she overextends herself: the duel will be between Dad and my aunt.

Dad gets more beer. Now he drinks directly out of the bottle, and for once Grandma does not object. She has her eyes on her estate; manners are no longer that important.

We go our rounds.

Someone presses money into my hand under the table. It is Aunt Sylvia, and she winks. I see from her glance that she wants me to pass it on to Nick. A bribe for Park Place. I hand it to Dad, and he buys another set of houses for his green block. He is not yet safe.

Nick has to sell after visiting Grandma's hotels. I bid an outrageous sum for Park Place. Mom looks at me oddly. I know she must have added up my accounts. How can I afford it?

I came prepared to cheat. My pockets are stuffed with money borrowed from a boy in my class. I have come to let Dad win.

I find myself bidding against him and Aunt Sylvia.

"Kate, you can't want Park Place!" Aunt Sylvia looks at me, hurt.

Dad kicks me under the table.

I back out.

"Let the best man win," sighs Grandma Hofmann. Aunt Sylvia acquires Park Place and howls with joy.

Ten minutes later I tip over Dad's beer. The yellow flood sweeps away Grandma's hotels.

It is drastic, but it does end the game.

Aunt Sylvia claims she would have won, but so do Grandma, Dad, Nick, and I. Only Mom says she will talk with me later.

Later I am asleep.

TWELVE

"How did it go?" Kate asked Kriemhild at supper. She had
reported back to Maren with the limp excuse of having lost
them, which had earned her another demerit.

"Guess where we were hiding."

"In the duck pond, breathing through straws," said Kate.

"Not bad," the twin conceded. "Have another guess."

"In the family tomb of the graveyard. There is one, isn't
there?"

Kriemhild shook her head.

"I give up."

"Remember the gang of prisoners in the big field? They
hardly catch the eye, do they? We played them! We posed
as prisoners, wrapped in our blankets. Six of us hoed, two
were guards, and the rest were flat on their stomachs. Your
team passed us at close range, and nobody even looked
twice. Then that fool Trudy gave us away. She squealed
when a fieldmouse whizzed over her chest."

"She didn't wear her jade-green blanket, did she?" Kate
was laughing.

So the duel between Maren and Sylvia was not over yet.

There was instruction scheduled for the evening, and
Maren was hanging the map of Europe in the center of the

wall. Instruction could be either the study of party history or the life of one of their leaders or martyrs. Or the discussion of an important speech or slogan or new directives. Or the progress of the war.

"My father is fighting in southern Russia," said Inga. Bolshevik Russia took nearly one third of the map, dark bloody red on the right-hand side. It was bigger than any other country.

Everybody's father or brother or uncle or cousin was fighting somewhere. Kate followed her dad around the map, first Poland, light brown at Germany's eastern border; then Belgium, small and yellow at the western border; a few months in France, blue and as big as Germany; and now Prague, in what used to be Czechoslovakia and was now a German province. No, there was Norway too, in 1940, way on top of the map, light blue like the snow and ice up there.

Ose said her father had died in the fighting near Leningrad, and Maren pointed to the northeastern corner of the map and asked them to stand at attention for two minutes. They stood, silent.

Frokke said her brother Frank had been captured in North Africa and was now at a prisoner-of-war camp in England. This time they did not stand in silence. Frokke shouldn't have talked about it, Kate thought. To be taken prisoner was shameful. It didn't happen to German soldiers. Or very rarely.

Maren began telling them about an ancient battle that sounded much like their afternoon arrow hunt, except that the Germanic tribes had wiped out the barbarians, who had disclosed their true low nature by impersonating animals, slipping into the hides of goats.

Just then Sylvia bounded into the room and swung into one of her flying ace stories Kate knew so well and didn't mind listening to in her anonymity. Sylvia talked about parachuting into partisan-held country in Yugoslavia and pretending to be local peasants till the German ground forces relieved them. The story sounded absolutely authentic, and Kate would have sworn that for the most part it was true.

"You must have dyed your hair," Kriemhild said into the hushed room.

"Gosh, kid, I didn't go along—I'm not allowed to, not yet—but I'd dye my hair and masquerade and deceive and do *anything* because I think some people are superior and have a right to win no matter what."

Maren's, as well as Sylvia's story too, Kate thought, was supposed to bolster their fighting spirit for the night raid.

"Why does it have to be at night?" moaned Kriemhild later on, yawning. They were dressing in gym suits instead of pajamas and sheets. "Why not an early morning attack?"

"I'd hate that," said Kate, who liked to sleep long but usually was awakened by the mother's helper groping for her clothing when it was still dark.

"Light gives us away," Marianne declared, testing the knot in her towel.

Ose tied her black neckerchief across her nose and mouth.

"You look scary! Let's all do it," Inga said.

But Trudy's neckerchief kept slipping down, and Kriemhild said she couldn't breathe under the cloth. They drifted outside.

Brunhild dipped her towel into the trough and hung it over the arm of the avenging angel. All the other girls did the same, so that the war memorial looked like a scarecrow. The village kids gawked and wondered aloud what was going on, but nobody answered them, so they melted away into the falling night.

Sigrid played her recorder, and they sang to pass the time. One song followed the other, and they knew a lot of songs. Sylvia's voice rang out. Kate wished she could carry a tune as well as her sister, but she usually was off-key and totally lost in a round.

Then a staff car pulled onto the green and stopped smartly in front of the group.

"Have a good time! I'll cross my fingers. You're going to win!" Sylvia was about to get into the limousine.

"Aren't you going with us?"

"We're counting on you!"

"You can't leave now!"

"Orders," she said curtly, and was gone.

"But we were planning to attack in two teams," cried Marianne and Inga.

"Frokke is leading the second team." Maren sounded sharp.

Maren and Frokke were the only persons not disappointed by Sylvia's departure, Kate thought. And it *was* strange of her to leave right now.

Maren started another song, but the girls let it die. The last hour they waited in silence, listening to the sleepy sounds of the village—a dog growling, the calls of a nightbird, the hum and flutter of insects.

Maren reminded them once more of the route. "We take the Gatow road and turn right after leaving the village. It's a dirt road that runs between fields before it enters the forest.

Let's go or we won't be there by midnight. It's less than two miles.''

It was pitch-black as they set out in two groups, Maren first and Frokke two minutes later. They had been told that the moon would rise soon, and orders were to stick close to the girl in front or even hold on to her towel.

"And not a sound! And no flashlights!''

Kate and the twins let their group pass by at the turnoff. They could hear the slurping noise of the sneakers on the rough ground.

"What was that?'' Kate thought she saw someone move at their flank. A wolf circling a herd of sheep? Harelipped Harry spying, as seemed to be his habit? Dead wood crackled, leaves rustled.

"What? Where?'' The talkative twin was gripping Kate's arm. "I don't see anything.''

Brunhild pulled them forward. Someone tried to suppress a cough, a giggle. A call for order was hissed. The shadow was gone.

They lingered a moment at the edge of the wood, the lane now the blackest tunnel. There was the twitter of a bird and the high, piercing cry of a rodent. Kate felt both twins twitch.

"I hate the dark,'' whispered Kriemhild.

Trudy moaned and was silenced. "Hush . . .''

The footsteps ahead surely were the other girls'. . . .

Later the clearing seemed almost bright. Kate could see the dark mass of the hostel against the lighter gray forty yards away. Here they met up with the first group, and for the longest time nothing happened.

Maren should give the signal to advance, Kate thought.

Her legs were heavy; she felt like stamping. The other girls were becoming restless, too. There was louder breathing. Uneasy, erratic jiggling traveled through the groups. They were really waiting far too long.

"Maren! Maren!" whispered urgent voices. "Maren, where are you?"

Maren was not there.

"I thought she was next to you."

"Maren, where are you?"

Suddenly triumphant laughter burst from the building and resounded over the clearing. It roared from every window of the hostel, stopped when a whistle screeched and an arrogant voice announced, "We've captured your leader. She will be our prisoner. We will deal with her and you tomorrow. Now we are going to sleep. Good night and Heil Hitler!"

"That's not true!" shouted Frokke.

"You're lying! You must be lying!" came angry cries from Kate and her comrades.

Then Maren spoke up, halting but still determined, asking them to go back to their camp.

"Frokke will lead," she said, and then they heard a window close.

"They must have kidnaped her right in front of the building."

"Grabbed her before she could cry out! They tricked her!"

"Let's free her now!"

"We'll storm the hostel!"

As one phalanx, they crashed against the door. Kate threw herself against the wood, hammered on windows, shouted at the top of her lungs. We lost Maren, she thought. It's as shameful as losing our flag, our honor. And the hostel kids insult us by refusing to fight. As if we weren't *worth* fighting. She flung herself again at the door.

The kids in the building jeered at them from the upper floor, dropped refuse, and in the end sloshed them with buckets full of water.

"Good night," they called, and all windows were banged shut.

When they retreated, the moon had come up, and all the dogs in the area were howling. It was a sad retreat.

About an hour later, when Sylvia barged into the dormitory, she found them gloomy and crestfallen, and it took a lot of listening and encouraging and planning before they were willing to go to bed.

"Isn't she marvelous," said Marianne, and everybody sighed.

The ransom note was pinned to the door of the school in the morning. "RANSOM," it said in big black letters, and Frokke saw it when she went to wash. It called them a lot of names, like "subject population," "vassals," "subjugated subjects."

"As if we were Polish or Russian," said Ose, furious.

And it spelled out the demands they would have to meet if they wanted their leader back.

"Four pounds of chamomile, one pound of dried white nettle, five pounds each of raspberry, blackberry, coltsfoot, tansy, narrow-leaved plantain, mint, and woodruff." Frokke was reading out loud, and with the listing of each new plant her voice rose to a yelp.

"The bastards!"

"They can't do that!"

"Woodruff! They're crazy—the season for woodruff is over!"

"What about Maren? What do we do?"

They talked back and forth, Frokke white and tense, others red with fury and excitement. Kate was not even thinking about filling the ridiculous demands. "Come on! We'll liberate her right now!"

The twins twirled their knotted towels, and Ose and Inga squared their shoulders.

"Let's not rush into anything," Frokke cautioned.

At breakfast Marianne and some of the others appealed to Sylvia. Sylvia calmly told them not to worry; her plan was ready.

"We need a negotiator, one of you to go to the hostel with a white flag to talk it out," she said. There were no volunteers, because it wasn't exactly a job that piled honor on you, Kate thought. Then her name was called.

"What about you, Kate Hofmann?" asked Sylvia.

"All right." Kate stood erect and stared straight ahead. Her sister was going to need her in the rescue operation, she thought. It was her duty to help, but she wasn't happy about it.

"Wear your uniform," Frokke instructed her.

"Yes."

Hiking along the dirt road to the hostel, Kate felt miserable. The buttoned-up pea jacket was far too warm, and her tightly knotted neckerchief was stifling her. The white flag, fashioned from a broomstick and a pillow case, underlined her wretched task. The talking twin had argued that waving a dish towel when Kate approached the hostel would be quite enough to signal negotiations, but Sylvia had demanded a real flag. As if her sister had remembered Kate's lament about never being allowed to carry the flag of her Berlin unit, Kate thought darkly. She would have been glad to have even Harry's company.

"Stop!"

The hostel crowd was expecting her, and three of them escorted her inside, smirking. She was put into an office and told to wait. And wait she did, upright, holding the awful flag, her face blank.

The sound of a motor drew her to the window. A staff car was pulling up with Harry on the running board. He had leaped off and opened the door before the driver emerged. He let out Sylvia, decked out as a very high-ranking Hitler Youth leader. Her hair was pulled back and twisted into a bun at the back of her neck. Her dark skirt was rather long, and she wore glasses and carried a briefcase. She looked thoroughly official, and Kate felt flushed with admiration. She saw Sylvia's lips move, and the kids lingering outside snapped to attention. Then Sylvia walked into the building and seconds later entered the office.

"Heil Hitler." Kate was ignored except for a curt glance.

Leaders and subleaders came to report.

Sylvia showed just the right amount of interest, Kate observed. While Sylvia delivered in a warden's voice a monologue on doing one's duty, serving the people, the boys and girls stared straight ahead. Sylvia went on and on about the war effort; all work, she said, was equally important, and if the Führer asked you to gather plants, then you should excel at picking plants—it was your duty and the German people depended on you. She asked how they were doing and said that she would like to see the building. They should not think of it as an inspection.

"I will talk to all the campers later. Have them fall in for roll call under the flag." She fumbled with her briefcase. "I brought one or two citations."

Commands were issued, whistles blown.

Sylvia made a leisurely tour through the hostel, even going so far as to taste the soup in the kitchen. Nobody held Kate back when she trailed her. And she followed her sister outside where the two groups, girls and boys separated, stood at rigid attention. Kate discovered Maren in the back row, shepherded by two husky girls.

Again Sylvia talked about duty and obedience and service and the fatherland, and she pumped the hands of two boys and one girl and pinned a badge on their shirts.

"*Sieg!*" she shouted.

"*Heil!*" was the shouted answer.

Three times the *Sieg Heil* rang across the clearing. It was a great performance, thought Kate.

Half turned toward the car, Sylvia said that she was passing through Gatow. "Is there anything I can do for anyone?"

It should have been Maren's clue, but there was no reply.

Kate stepped forward. Here finally was her turn to assist. "How about a ride into Decherow?"

"That's a stone's throw away. I wasn't offering support to the lazy."

The assembled kids snickered, and Kate stood stonily. She hoped she wasn't blushing. It was part of Sylvia's act, she knew, but it was hard to be made fun of.

Now Maren caught on and asked faintly to be taken into Gatow. "To telephone home in an emergency," she said.

Sylvia beckoned her to the car, and Harry ushered them both inside. Then he was ordered to step back.

"By the way"—Sylvia was leaning out of her window, the glasses gone now—"greetings from Camp Decherow, and my advice is to have a closer look at those badges before flaunting them around." She gave a mock salute and the car sped off.

"I was expendable and so were you," Harry told Kate as they wandered under the trees. They had dashed for the woods in the wild hubbub after Sylvia's departure. "She didn't need a 'local guide' any more or a—why were you there anyway?"

Kate didn't hear him.

"But don't you see she had to let them know they had been taken in? That they had been fooled, fake badges and all? That our camp won? Besides, she knows I'm a pretty good runner."

He went on. "I wouldn't have liked to be in your shoes if they'd caught you. And I feel sorry for the other girl."

"Well, I'm sort of glad I don't have to look at Maren," Kate confessed. "But without Sylvia she'd still be locked up."

Harry cocked his head. "Would she?"

For a fleeting moment Kate wondered what her sister had been up to last night. Then she looked around.

"We aren't on our way back to the village, are we?" she asked. "They don't expect me at camp right away."

"Glashagen Spring?"

"Mind if I come?"

He grinned. "But you have to get rid of that."

"That" was the white flag she had been clutching all along. She tossed it on the ground and covered it with leaves.

THIRTEEN

◇ "Stop here, please," says Aunt Sylvia.

The car lurches and brakes to a halt.

Aunt Sylvia directs Dad to park in a narrow slot between vans. It is Wednesday evening, and we have been doing another of the required memory tours. Mom said she wouldn't endure another one. It was unfair, too, since she couldn't pay Aunt Sylvia back with *her* line of old schools, old apartments, old tennis courts, old coffee houses, old parks, and old street corners. All her childhood places had been wiped out.

I think Aunt Sylvia is glad Mom doesn't come along.

So it is she and Dad in front and Grandma Hofmann and Bozo and I in the back seat. Nick excused himself with homework, and I could have done the same. Instead I have been "difficult" and "negative" all afternoon.

We stop where we have never stopped before.

"But this isn't where your friend Nicola used to live," says Grandma.

"Look over there, everybody."

I see a wall of people, police vehicles, floodlights, red flags.

"A demonstration," I say.

"Let's have a look." Aunt Sylvia climbs out of the car.

"Radicals, communists, anarchists, and troublemakers," mutters Grandma, and lodges herself firmly into her corner. Her cheeks quiver with disapproval.

Aunt Sylvia, Dad, Bozo, and I shoot across the square.

"Look at the banners!"

The red cloth unfurls, and there are swastikas.

"Neo-Nazis," I say.

The line of spectators is only three deep, and I burrow through. In the street are perhaps two hundred men. They are wearing brown uniforms and high boots and caps strapped across their chins. There are leather belts running diagonally down their chests, which make them look martial, and red arm bands with swastikas sewn to their sleeves. Their boots are strong and polished. Torches are handed around.

I edge over to Dad and Aunt Sylvia. Bozo wheezes.

"Storm troopers," she says. "I wonder. . . ." Her eyes dart over the scene. She spots the cameras, the director, the makeup men.

"A movie!" she cries. "Look at the old-fashioned cars and bikes!"

"It takes you right back, doesn't it?" An elderly man joins in. "People came up all afternoon for a look, and they were upset."

"It's so real. Look at the street lamps, the advertising, the store windows! They fixed up the street! Very clever, isn't it?"

"A time warp," I say. "Folks, you're now back in 1943."

"What do you know about it, a kid like you! 1943? More like 1933, when Hitler came to power. Look at the clothes, the suits and coats the extras are wearing, the Jewish names above the shops."

The director comes running with his megaphone. Orders are barked. The storm troopers stand in formation.

"One, two—a song!" bellows the leader, and the company sings with unsure voices. I make out something about Aryan blood.

"No punch behind it," declares Aunt Sylvia, one fist beating into the palm of her hand. The song is repeated.

"Too soft, too soft," she mutters, and I am afraid that the next time she will lead the singing.

Dad talks technical stuff with the elderly man and his wife. They turn out to be in the business and know about how to procure boots, uniforms, props. Dad loves technical details.

"Are you saying that—"

"Attention!" The bullhorn is telling the storm troopers what to do to extinguish their torches. An assistant demonstrates, dipping his burning torch into a pail of water and dropping it into a metal drum.

"A pair of boots costs forty-five dollars, and they still have the formula for the storm trooper brown dye," reports Dad.

The storm troopers mill around. In real life they are accountants, teachers, electricians, shopkeepers, train conductors, civil service workers, ministers.

"They hired a church choir," the elderly man explains.

Now the torches are lighted. The men stand in formation; in front there are two rows with large banners. The director circles them for a final inspection. Then the command is shouted.

"One, two . . . a song!"

The flames blaze, the men sing and march. Their marching is atrocious. They cannot keep step. Some are slow, some fast, others stumble. The bystanders laugh; Aunt Sylvia laughs the loudest. They do look ridiculous. But at least they've gotten the hang of the song.

Bozo streaks after them and attacks one of the flags. He returns with a mouthful of red cloth.

"What took you so long?" Grandma Hofmann sniffs in her corner.

"A time warp," I say. Bozo lets go of his trophy. The flags were so much redder than I had imagined them.

FOURTEEN

July 6, 1943

It was late afternoon when Kate walked across the green. A motorcycle had pulled up at the school. Her comrades were lined up in the yard, and Kate slipped behind the door and peered outside. A strange young woman, a very high-ranking leader, was pacing in front of them, talking.

"Your leader, Maren, has been called home on urgent family matters," she said, and Kate speculated—a bombed-out apartment? A relative wounded or dead?

"Sylvia Hofmann has agreed to take Maren's job in this emergency. We are all thankful to Sylvia—" Here the girls interrupted, cheering. "We at the area office know that Sylvia has the capacity for leadership. We have full confidence in her." Again the girls cheered, and Kate felt her heart suddenly sink. It was an odd and uncomfortable feeling.

Then Sylvia addressed the group in her official warden's voice, looking enthusiastic and competent. She ended with the news that she was planning a variety show for the village.

"And for the kids at the Youth Hostel," she said, "folk dancing, singing, recorders, charades, riddles, magic, sketches."

There was clapping.

"But we won't forget our duty. We promise to fill our quota a hundred and fifty percent, don't we?"

This time there was roaring applause. Sylvia had won their solid vote. Kate watched Frokke come forward and shake Sylvia's hand.

That was when Kate went up to the attic. The air was heavy with heat and the pungent smell of the drying plants. Kate emptied her two bags. She could see that the others had been idle. Slowly, carefully, she spread out her harvest.

First Harry and she had gone to Glashagen Spring and built a fire and brewed tea, as they had the day before. Only today there had been raw vegetables, carrots and peas for lunch, and cake, too—a large flat square with browned, melted sugar on top, a bit stale and suspiciously like the one Sylvia had cut up as a snack yesterday. Kate had eaten the cake without asking about it, and she had not demanded to see his secret cache, though he seemed to be well-supplied.

Kate respected his privacy. She hated it when her mother or Belinda went through her belongings, and she had always envied Sylvia's possession of the desk with the secret compartments.

"I told everybody about this . . . dream tank," Kate had teased Harry, waving her hand into the diffuse green light, and she could still see the blood seep out of his face and only the scar turn a perverse pink.

"You didn't!"

"I didn't," she had assured him. "But you never made me promise." She had told him about the elaborate vows she and her sister used and that she would never break one of them.

"A propeller!" He had thought that funny. "A piece of wood!

"But why?" he had asked then. "Don't you trust each other?" He didn't seem to understand that loyalties could shift and that some oaths were sacred and others less so and could be easily overridden.

"That's why we pledge allegiance to the flag. The number-one oath. Don't they teach you anything here? Aren't you a member of the Hitler Youth?"

As an answer Harry had turned his face toward Kate.

They had talked about the aborted attack on the hostel last night. "They were lying in wait for us, as if they'd been told we were coming."

Harry had confided that he had shadowed them. "You didn't see me, did you?"

Kate had waited for him to go on.

"I watched you and the twins pause at the turnoff. Later I scared all of you, shrieking." He had given his rodent cry.

"One of you ran into a tree."

That had been Trudy.

"What else?"

"Earlier I listened to you sing on the green, and I followed a small boy with a note up to the Youth Hostel."

"Before the car drove up." Kate had seen it happen: Sylvia talking to a village kid near the memorial and the boy shooting off the green.

"But why would she do it?" Kate had asked, feeling dull and heavy. It *was* Sylvia who had set up the trap for Maren.

"Maybe all she cares about is herself," Harry had said. "You like her, so watch out."

Abruptly Kate had gotten up. "I want to pick plants."

"I know an abandoned rifle range," Harry had said. "It's the right kind of soil for chamomile."

Running with Harry through the woods, Kate had soon lost all sense of direction. They had skirted tracts of light green larches, schools of pines, wet, soggy bogs. They had crossed overgrown, unused lanes, faint animal tracks, and a slow creek. There had been no deer and no wild pigs, only the banging of woodpeckers. Once he had paused and checked a road before waving her across, and she had known it was the road to the prisoner-of-war camp.

Then the trees had ended. Unruly thick long grass, mixed with red clover and rabbit-foot, plantain and yarrow, covered the ground. On the first bank Kate could see the white and yellow chamomile. And masses of blackberries. "It's all mine," Harry had said, half serious. "The villagers don't come here any more, and they used to gather the nuts and berries."

He had shown her the hazelnuts, still green and soft; the elderberry bushes weighed down with unripe fruit; the clumps of raspberry canes and the wild strawberry plants. There were three trenches, separated by grassy dams, running straight against a wall. Harry had kept his voice down.

"Sounds travel," he had said.

So the prison camp was close. Kate had felt her heart stumble, and she had plunged into collecting chamomile as if to pay for her trespassing. Harry helped her. Once she had been startled by fierce whistling.

"Can you see it?"

"The camp? From the top of the far slope."

So he had seen it.

The humming of the bees was deafening.

"Do you like to collect shells? We could dig for them up there where the target used to be." Harry gestured to the end of the trench.

"No, thanks, not today."

They had left when their bags had been filled and their hands dyed brown with chamomile juice. All the way back Kate had sniffed at them. The woods had remained empty. Only at the state forest road they had waited, concealed in the underbrush, for an army truck to rumble past.

"Prisoners?"

"Guards."

The barrels of guns had been visible.

In the attic now, Kate tended the beds of drying plants, turning them over tenderly. Then she went down.

Again she was late. The girls were sitting at supper, and Kate gulped as she saw her bowl full of a glutinous pudding with a leathery skin. Sylvia made Kate report, and while Kate stood at attention, Sylvia gave a lecture on deportment. At home Sylvia was late three times out of five and hardly ever bothered to excuse herself, Kate thought, her eyes fixed on the disgusting skin.

"Hold up your hands," Sylvia ordered, and Kate exhibited her dark stained palms.

"Yak!"

The girls bubbled over with laughter. Kate saw open mouths, flushed faces, and concentrated on her pudding, although she did hear Sylvia ordering her to scrub the hall later.

"To teach you to eat with clean hands. Dismissed!"

Her sister needed someone easy to practice leadership on, she thought as she went to her seat. Right now she was concerned only with the pudding. It looked ghastly. No amount of self-discipline would help her get it down, Kate was sure. She picked up her spoon and felt all eyes staring at her as she broke the skin. With a smacking sound the pudding plopped apart. It was lumpy throughout. Kate, despairing, cast about for help—to Sylvia with Marianne and Ose, her new adjutants, at the head of the table; to Sigrid and Inga and Frokke, anxious for her to finish supper; to the twins, scraping their bowls; to Olga, mute in a corner; to the flag and the Führer, gazing placidly out of his golden frame. Her jaws felt locked, she told Harry later.

"Screwed together," she described it.

All of a sudden she took her bowl and walked out with it. She dumped the pudding into the slop pail.

"And the funny thing was I felt as if I had won," she told Harry. "Though it's perfectly plain that I lost, isn't it? I can't explain it."

"I don't get it." Harry was puzzled. "Is that what you learn at your meetings?"

The incident was passed over. There was a murmur of voices in the room when Kate returned to eat her sandwich.

After supper she scrubbed the hallway and listened to her sister carrying out her first evening of instruction. Sylvia was swinging into the life of Field Marshal Hermann Göring, the party celebrity she knew best. She talked about his flying ace days in World War I with the Red Baron, his early friendship with Adolf Hitler. And she mentioned her own father, a minor flying ace but the field marshal's buddy. It did explain the staff cars and her flight stories, thought Kate, but she had orphaned Kate by claiming Dad for herself only. There was awed silence.

"So you must have seen the Führer too," Marianne murmured reverently.

Once at a reception she had been allowed to present flowers, Sylvia said.

"It was wonderful. . . ." She had to grope for words. "I . . . he . . . the Führer . . . if he had asked me to die for him . . ."

Kate stopped scrubbing and sat on her haunches.

It was the talkative twin who broke the spell in the classroom. "We could play that scene in our show—the grand finale could be a pageant."

Kate heard muted talking.

"And who is going to play . . . him?"

Again it was quiet.

"Why not use the gigantic oil painting?" Kate had popped her head through the doorway, and the girls swiveled toward the portrait.

Sylvia nodded thoughtfully.

"Great! That's it!" shouted Kriemhild.

"Sylvia, let's do that. It sounds wonderful," called Marianne, and Ose said, "A beautiful ending."

"I had a bunch of flowers—wild flowers—poppies, larkspur, Queen Ann's lace, wisps of rye and wheat, cornflowers. They're his favorite." Sylvia gazed around the room. "I can see it—a group of you in uniform. I step forward and place the flowers on the floor. We sing and the curtain falls—it sounds marvelous." She flashed a smile at Kate.

Everybody clamored for a part in the pageant.

"I think you'll all agree we should take only girls with blond hair," Sylvia said. That left out Kate and the twins and half the others. Kate didn't care; she was thinking of what she would do—her very own act in the limelight.

"There has to be a Maypole dance," Inga proposed.

"Sigrid and I could do a duet on the recorder." That was Frokke.

Everybody was offering suggestions, ideas, talents.

"What about a poem?"

"My sister and I have a funny routine. We do it at home on New Year's Eve."

"I will do my magic act," said Sylvia during a lull. "It's my specialty."

Kate felt as if she had been punched in the stomach; she gasped for air. *Sylvia's specialty?*

It was Kate who knew all sorts of magic tricks, not her sister. Like making secret ink and pulling coins out of the air and surprising her audience with mumbo-jumbo illusions and card tricks. All through the winter Kate had worked at perfecting her repertoire. And now she was being robbed. She was angry.

"Show us something."

"Do some magic tricks, Sylvia!"

"Can you make a rabbit jump out of a hat?"

"Or a Houdini? A locked-box mystery?"

Sylvia stood there smiling, and only Kate knew that she could perform just one single magic act. Although she did that one extremely well, Kate had to admit.

"Not now"—Sylvia warded them off—"or you won't be surprised. Who wants to be my assistant?"

All hands but Kate's were up instantly, and as Sylvia's eyes traveled through the room, Kate knew she would be called. Her sister needed her.

"Kate Hofmann."

"No," she said. "I don't want to."

The girls stared at her as if she had declined a medal. At first they were startled and then rather hostile, Kate thought. And Sylvia looked bewildered, and her upper lip quivered when she asked Frokke to be her assistant, as if Kate had hurt her, instead of the other way around.

Dutiful Frokke bellowed an enthusiastic, "Yes!"

"Brunhild and I need a third partner," whispered Kriemhild as the girls flocked around their leader.

Kate had astonished herself. She wasn't used to saying no to her sister.

FIFTEEN

◇ We are sitting at supper. Supper is cold meat and cheese and salad and bread with butter, and tea, wine, and beer. Aunt Sylvia says she loves a German supper.

Dad tells Aunt Sylvia that I am chairman of the middle school centennial celebration committee. He sounds proud.

"Our old school!" he says with feeling.

"Yeah, with Kate the great stage manager," Nick chimes in. I can handle him. A kick under the table will quiet him instantly. But Dad is another story. He considers himself my friend, and he cannot understand that he's assuming the impossible. A parent cannot be a friend, I am certain.

"How wonderful, Katie darling! What are you doing? What are you planning? Tell me all about it! Can I drop in on one of your meetings?" asks Aunt Sylvia. She, too, believes she is my friend.

"You do meet tomorrow after school, don't you?" says Dad.

"Mind if I come?" asks Aunt Sylvia.

I shrug, already feeling nauseous. Maybe I'll develop a fever.

"Don't you think we'd better leave the kids alone?" Mom says, too low.

Nobody hears her. Anyway, it is three to one against her. For there is Grandma Hofmann.

"Kate will be glad if you come, Sylvia," she states firmly.

How does she know?

Grandma is too old to change her mind about raising children. "I don't care about all your newfangled theories," I have heard her say. "Children have to obey. You're your child's best friend? Poppycock!"

I like her for it. At least it is clear that we are on opposite sides.

"And where do I go?" inquires Aunt Sylvia.

"Room 29 in the new wing."

Nick watches me calmly. He knows I am lying. There is no Room 29.

All through the next morning I feel my forehead. It remains cool. I raise my hand, I answer questions, I am a student.

After school my friends and the other members of the cast drift into the music room. I watch the door.

Werner escorts Aunt Sylvia and Bozo into the room.

My friends greet her. They haven't forgotten the bowling and the food. They remember the scar on her arm and the train robbery on Machu Picchu.

"Hello, Kate's aunt," they call. She likes it. I know she'd like it even better if they simply called her Sylvia.

"Well, hello!" She sparkles. "I'll sit quietly in this corner. . . ."

I know she won't be quiet for long. There is the agenda. Besides, my friends won't let her stay excluded.

Werner and Berga are beginning to show off.

"Guess who we're supposed to be, Kate's aunt," they exclaim. We are working on a takeoff on the school's history. We have studied the school yearbooks in the branch library.

Werner strokes his phantom mustache. He is Emperor Wilhelm I, under whose reign the school was founded. He is the guest of honor at the opening and gives an inane patriotic speech to the student body, male only at that time. Berga is the student body. One can see the tight collar that squeezes her head up and back.

"Oh, you're so clever!" Aunt Sylvia wipes tears of laughter from her cheeks.

"We call it 'Hysteric Review,' " I say. I thought of it, and I still like it.

"Oh, you're so clever," my aunt repeats. "All I ever did with my Girl Scouts were songs and dances and charades and magic."

"Magic?"

"Why don't you show us something?"

"Make that ugly dog disappear!"

"Do a Houdini! Make yourself disappear!"

I start laughing, and Werner prods me, but I can't stop.

Grandma told us about the time Sylvia slipped out of her Hitler Youth uniform into an evening gown, "Singing that foreign jazz for the American soldiers," Grandma said. "Sylvia was always one for coming out on top. She has a beautiful voice—she could have been a famous singer if she hadn't married John and gone to the United States as one of the first war brides."

She did a Houdini all right.

SIXTEEN

July 7, 1943

"Theft is a heinous, unforgivable crime against all the people, against the German nation as a whole." Sylvia pronounced every word distinctly. In two tiers the girls formed a ring around the flagpole, and Sylvia went around each circle, pausing and staring hard into each and every face. Kate saw Marianne swallow nervously. Sigrid and Ose flushed bright red, and the twins were gnawing their lips.

"Who goes against his comrades places himself outside their community," said Sylvia, and studied her sister, and Kate could have sworn that the three loaves of bread that had been reported missing by Olga were hidden in her backpack; she felt that guilty. Then she blinked and boldly stared back. Why should she steal three loaves? And nobody would walk across the green with arms full of bread.

Suddenly she remembered Harry pushing a wheelbarrow laden with hay past the school. It had happened an hour ago, when she was brushing her teeth near the pump. It would have been easy for Harry to spirit the bread away.

"A German youth does not steal." Sylvia now faced Trudy, and Trudy trembled. "Go check your stuff to see if anything else is gone and report back in fifteen minutes. Dismissed!"

There was a rush for the door, and then the girls went rummaging through their backpacks and bedrolls.

"Three loaves of bread. I bet it's that Olga!"

"Where's my whistle?"

"Who's seen my pocketknife?"

"I *know* I brought a bathing cap."

"My toothbrush!"

"Who'd take your toothbrush, Kriemhild?"

"My soap, my lilac soap! I can't find it!"

"Sigrid did bring soap! Why don't you ever use it?"

In the end they came up with a report of what was missing—a pocketknife, Sigrid's mess kit, marked S.S. for Sigrid Seifert, and a flashlight out of Sylvia's huge trunk. Kate knew the flashlight well. It worked without batteries; you pumped a handle. It was quite valuable, considering the constant shortages, although it wasn't easy to read by its light under a blanket. She and her sister had both begged their dad for it.

When none of the girls volunteered, Sylvia had to appoint a search party to go through everybody's belongings. "I know it's an unpleasant duty," she said, and called on Frokke and Kate. "A Hofmann for a Hofmann's luggage."

The girls twittered gratefully.

It was indiscreet but interesting, thought Kate, combing first through her sister's and then through some of the other kids' stuff. Frokke worked methodically, and Kate saw her flipping through letters and diaries. "We aren't looking for words, are we?" Kate said. She watched her closely as Frokke, eyes narrowed, examined her backpack.

"You leave my notebook alone." Kate put it into her shoulder bag.

Sylvia had two pictures of Werner Grasshof: one in goggles, flying cap, and white scarf, waving out of a plane, and a portrait, showing perfect teeth in a dazzling smile. Marianne carried a rosary in the pocket of her pea jacket. Sigrid's clothing was as filthy as Kate had expected. Kriemhild did own another pair of shoes beside the ridiculous pumps, and Frokke had stowed a half-eaten sausage at the bottom of her pack. She blushed angrily when Kate held it up.

"Nothing," Frokke informed Sylvia, and Sylvia flashed her smile and told the girls to go foraging for the rest of the morning.

"You're on your own," she said, letting them go.

Small groups banded together.

"Kate, show us where you got your chamomile yesterday!"

Kate shook her head.

"Gee, we're comrades, aren't we?"

They were angry, she knew, but she couldn't betray Harry. Besides, the range was off limits. None of the girls asked her to join a group, and she waited by herself till they had marched off. Then she went out on the green.

Prisoners were building a stage next to the war memorial. One of the guards had slung his rifle over the angel's arm; a second guard aimed his rifle carelessly at the men. Both were calling out automatically, "Quick, quick, Ivan, hurry up."

The prisoners were slow. Kate watched their sluggish movements—how they staggered along with a wooden board, how they took their time driving in a nail. It was only when the elderly guard threw them some bread that they hustled to get at it. Like animals.

"Hello there." Harry, visored cap drawn down over his face, had detached himself from his observation post behind the war memorial. "The others took the Bollhagen road."

"They don't want me along."

"I'm on my way to the rifle range. Want to come?" asked Harry. He understood about not being wanted.

"Sure."

This time Kate memorized how to get there. The range was the same as it had been the day before. Bees hummed importantly. Spiderwebs were suspended between bushes. The sun was warm on the grass, and there was the lazy smell of summer. Clouds of small black flies wavered in midair.

"We'll take it easy today and collect only blackberry leaves." Kate had brought two bags, and they picked side by side. There was no special sound from the camp.

"What can you see from up there?" She pointed to the far slope.

"Barracks and watchtowers and barbed wire. And the prisoners and their guards."

"Did you go close?"

Harry nodded. "Close enough to throw things over the fence. It's a bad place."

She was startled by the way he spit out the words.

Then the bags were full and their hands scratched and bloody.

"Tea?" he asked.

"Yes, tea."

The hike seemed to be shorter. They tumbled into the hollow over one of the steep walls, slipping and sliding.

Kate sat on the steps as before, and Harry went for pot and mugs and kindling wood. When he dunked the pot into the pool, she saw that she had been right. It was Sigrid's mess tin. Inscribed into the paint and soot was "S.S." Why didn't he have sense enough to rub it out? she thought.

Harry made tea—a mixture of mint and strawberry leaves—and served it with bread and sausage, his ugly face twisted with pleasure.

"You like it?" he kept repeating eagerly. "Mint and strawberry—they go well together, I think."

Kate nodded. Sylvia hadn't talked about a stolen sausage, she was sure. She took another bite. Probably Frokke had brought two and had been too ashamed of having kept them for herself to report the loss. Now Kate and Harry were sharing her sausage. Kate grinned at Harry. Sure, she would have to do something about the pilfering, but not now, not in the dream tank refuge.

"More tea, please," she said.

"What about the stage?" he asked, munching. Kate decided that she'd like him better if she didn't have to watch him eat. He did look his worst chewing with his chin dripping with spit.

"Oh, bringing culture to the peasants," she answered. "I'm going to do my magic tricks," she lied.

"Magic! I've never seen any."

Kate dug a coin out of her pocket and made it disappear, displaying her empty hands. He loved it when she zipped the coin out of his left ear. Then she whipped it out of his nose, the leg of his pants, his mug of tea. She was not that good, but he watched her every move.

"More," he said. Like Sven Peter, Kate thought.

"I'll be in the first row at the show to cheer," he promised.

"I'm not doing any magic," she confessed. "Sylvia is . . . she claims it's her specialty." Kate would have preferred to tell him the truth, but there was her promise.

"The greedy bitch," Harry said hotly. "I bet she stars in every single act, and you can't do anything because she's the leader and you've got to follow orders."

Kate liked him for his sympathy.

"I also know some card tricks," she said.

Like a shot he was gone and back with a pack of cards. It was a smudged but complete deck.

"So you play patience," Kate said, but he did not understand her.

"Do you play alone?"

He shook his head. "No, I don't play at all."

"So why do you have a deck of cards out here?"

For a moment she thought he was going to answer, but he didn't.

Kate did the four tricks she knew best. She repeated them at a slower pace. Then he took the playing cards, reshuffled them, bowed to her, and duplicated her act. He had grasped it much faster than anyone else she knew..

"Hey, you're great!" she said. "You're a natural—" She was going to say "actor" or "performer," but she caught herself in time. Not with his face.

Excited, he shuffled the cards more and more rapidly, conjured up a king, a queen of spades, a royal flush, stumbled over a pair of jacks, and in the end let the cards rain down on them. Laughing, Kate lolled on the steps.

Suddenly it was time to go, or she'd be late again. Kate

helped Harry clean up. Carrying mugs and teapot, she followed him around the temple. The back was more dilapidated. The paint had flaked off, but there was a real door, barricaded with a board. Harry opened it easily and walked in ahead.

The light was murky, but she saw right away that it was a beautifully stocked hideout. A pile of early potatoes in a corner. A primitive shelf with spring and early summer vegetables—beets, onions, carrots, two small heads of cabbage—old tin cans with what looked like sugar and salt, bags with various teas, labeled with care. On the bottom shelf the missing loaves of bread, a sausage. Another shelf with utensils, a second pot, more cracked mugs, chipped plates, matches, candles, a pocketknife, Sylvia's flashlight, a compass. There was a sort of bed on the floor, a heap of dry leaves and a blanket.

"Do you sleep here?"

"Not often." He was putting the mugs away.

A few pictures were thumbtacked to the walls. Kate studied them. A print of an antique landscape with a similar temple. A drawing of a man on a cross with a fat harelip. A soldier, a captain, older but as handsome as Werner Grasshof.

"My father," said Harry, waiting at the door.

Kate did not believe him. There was no likeness at all.

She fingered the pile of enemy leaflets, a lot more than she owned and some she had never seen. But there wasn't enough time now.

"I'll have to look through those when I come back tomorrow." Kate picked up Sylvia's flashlight and went past Harry. He watched her, shrugged lightly, and secured the door. He did not change color, and the scar did not turn pink.

They shouldered their bags and plunged downstream. Again they met nobody in the state forest, and it was only when they were close to Decherow that they ran into the gang of prisoners and their guards. It was too late to dodge.

"Quick, quick!" With sharp commands the prisoners were herded into the ditch to clear the road for Kate and Harry.

"The stage is all finished," the younger soldier called to her.

"Guess we're invited, aren't we?" The elderly one blocked their way.

"I'm sure you are." It was awkward to be stared at by so many eyes, Kate thought.

"Have to ask the group to sing my favorite—'Lilli Marlene.' "

The prisoners crouched in the ditch, impassive. Harry had stepped close, and one of them was slowly turning his head. Kate saw pockmarked, stubbly, gray skin, small dark, dull eyes, an incredibly dirty bandage, and for a moment a sharp interest, as if a message were being passed, and then the flicker of a true smile. He looked like Uncle Leo, she thought, Uncle Leo who wasn't a relative but a neighbor and who had stayed with her at the dentist's when he heard she was waiting alone to have a tooth pulled. The thought surprised her. It was treacherous.

"Let the villagers set up a sideshow!" The younger soldier grinned and gestured over to Harry. "Two-headed calves, chickens that can count—you know what I mean."

"One-armed mayors." Kate continued his list. Then she pulled Harry along.

The green was mobbed. The peasants, their kids, dogs, ducks, chickens, and Kate's comrades were swarming around the stage. Two horse-drawn carts had stopped short, now full of spectators, and the mayor sat high on his tractor. Kriemhild waved to Kate.

"Gosh, did you miss something! She's marvelous, Sylvia is! She's such a wonderful magician!"

Her sister was up on the stage, bowing, delighted, curls flying, with Frokke modestly a few steps back. So Sylvia couldn't even wait! She had to show off right away.

"Do it again!" begged one voice, and the crowd joined in. "Yes, do it again, do it again!"

The clamor grew, and Sylvia lifted both arms to quiet them. She showed a large green button and promised to let it disappear and retrieve it from someone else's pocket. She asked for volunteers. Everybody's arm shot up, and Sylvia searched the audience. For a second Kate was sure she was hunting for Harry, whose harelip would accentuate her own attractiveness, but when her sister invited the mayor to take part, Kate felt ashamed of her conjecture. Sylvia wasn't that small-minded.

The mayor lumbered stiffly onstage with two little girls, and Sylvia went through a routine of letting the button vanish in the palm of her hand and plucking it from sleeves, collars, ears, noses, mouths. The crowd was thrilled.

Sylvia was far from perfect; she was not even good. She bungled one trick completely, and the button plopped on the wooden stage and rolled into the trough. None of it mattered. The audience gasped at the right moments and in the end roared with applause. The mayor was crimson with pride when he climbed down.

"Wait for the real show! This is only a small preview," Kate heard the twin boast to the villager near her.

"Does anybody have a deck of cards?" Sylvia's voice pealed across the green.

Three, five, nine kids sped off. Five decks of cards were offered.

Sylvia did Kate's card tricks.

Again she did not do them well. Harry, with no practice, could do them almost as well, but everybody loved it. Kate clutched her bag of leaves and swallowed hard against the burning in her throat. Her sister had been terribly unfair, but she wasn't going to cry over a couple of magic tricks, not openly.

"You're so much better! She's lousy with the cards, but she knows how to play to the people. Look at the mayor still fawning." Harry nudged her.

Kate reached for his bag, turned abruptly, and marched into the school building. She climbed to the attic. She swallowed again, breathed deeply, then tended the drying plants. All of them had to be turned over or they would rot. The smell was intense and calming. Kate sat down and began writing in her notebook. She was a great recorder of facts and twice had to get up and peek through the attic window, once to make sure it was a lime tree and not a maple between the barns, and a second time to confirm that the avenging angel on top of the war memorial was raising his right arm like everybody else when shouting "Heil Hitler."

So she was very late for her kitchen duty.

SEVENTEEN

◇ Mrs. Malek has cleared away the luncheon dishes and swept the kitchen and left. Mom is finishing up an urgent order. Dad is at work, and Nick has gone to soccer practice. Grandma Hofmann is dozing with the curtains drawn, and Bozo is curled up in his basket, asleep.

I am sitting at the kitchen table, shelling walnuts. It is time for confessions, and I used to be a great one for blurting out family secrets.

Last year I told Aunt Sylvia that I hated my mother, that Mom preferred my brother, Nick, that she had let him go to the punk rock concert but not me. My aunt had listened and then hugged me. At supper she had broached the subject of my spending a year of junior high with her in the United States.

"I'd love to have Kate!" she had said. "We'll have a wonderful time together. Think of how her English will improve! And I've been all alone in this big house since John passed away."

Her husband has always figured only as "John who passed away."

Dad had seen the advantage at once.

Mom had mumbled about a generous offer.

Nick had been openly envious but scorned the idea of living with an aunt.

Grandma Hofmann had doubted I was worthy of such a privilege and said I had to earn it during the year.

For a moment I had felt betrayed by them, and I had avoided Mom's eyes. Then the idea of America, California, the desert, the surfing, Hollywood had overwhelmed me. I had gawked with pleasure.

Since May, since reading the journal, my school reports have taken a dive down. A year abroad is no longer talked about. A year in the United States wouldn't help my math and biology, would it?

There are bowls on the table, a chopping block, knives. Hard-boiled eggs and potatoes, onions and apples are arranged in separate clusters. Jars of cucumbers and beets stand waiting. Cream, mayonnaise, oil, salt and pepper have been rounded up. A plate of pickled herring dominates the center. "A type of fish you simply cannot find in California, or, as a matter of fact, anywhere in the United States," Aunt Sylvia is fond of exclaiming. She is preparing her famous Friday night herring salad. It is the only dish she does during her visit.

"You know your mother. She doesn't like anybody else in her kitchen. No woman does," she says.

I think of how often Dad developed his films in the sink, or Grandma Hofmann spilled her anise tea and cookie batter, or Nick cleaned and freshly oiled the different ball bearings of the bikes he fixes, of me, baking a cheesecake for my friends and brewing secret ink. I let it pass. Her comment is an invitation to confide.

Anyway, it's hard to contradict Aunt Sylvia.

She is peeling potatoes and cutting each one into neat little cubes.

"Your friend Werner is such a handsome boy. Do you see much of him?" She is trying another approach.

"He's okay." I try to crack two nuts with my bare hands.

"Let me!"

The shells splinter.

"Too bad Nick has such a heavy work schedule. Your father and I had a lot of fun together."

But my dad is twelve years younger than Aunt Sylvia. Did they really play hide-and-seek? Did they play Monopoly? I work furiously.

Aunt Sylvia chops the onions and adds them to the potatoes. She is dry-eyed. Onions do not make her eyes water.

"Your mother loves her work, doesn't she?"

"Yeah." I wonder if Grandma Hofmann complained to Aunt Sylvia about Mom's "Keep Out" sign on her door. She has established firm hours of work, and we respect them.

Aunt Sylvia cores and slices apples. She dices cucumbers and beets. Her hands move quickly and deftly.

"Your grandma is worried about you, Kate dear. You know how she fusses about manners and little things." She is still fishing.

"Grandma . . ." I sigh and shrug.

Aunt Sylvia snips at the fillets of fish. She sighs, companionable. Now it is her turn to confide.

"I couldn't live without these visits. No kidding. The older I get, the more important they are. Blood is thicker than water." She laughs comfortably and stirs the mixture in the bowl.

What about your sister? I want to ask. My friends said

direct questioning was the only fair method to get at the truth.

But why be fair?

"You remind me so much of Kate," Aunt Sylvia says suddenly. Her upper lip quivers. "We were very close, you know."

What if I have been wrong?

EIGHTEEN

🦅 *July 7, 1943*

At lunch Sylvia proclaimed the discovery of a number of elderberry bushes. "I couldn't believe my eyes—right at the edge of the village, untouched, loaded with fat green leaves. In one big effort we can fill our entire quota. We can be first in the district, perhaps even in the area. Isn't it wonderful?"

The girls broke into cheers.

"And the mayor agreed to deliver our stuff at the central collecting station in Gatow today. See you in the yard in five minutes. Dismissed!"

"What about kitchen duty?" Kate asked.

"We'll lock everything worth stealing into my room." It was obvious that she suspected Olga.

Out in the yard large bags of hemp normally used for grain were distributed. Then the girls marched off, singing, with Sylvia in the lead and three kids trailing. "We want to journey far across the field," they sang, and turned into the footpath between farms, along the open dung pit, the dried-out garden. At its end Sylvia went left for a hundred yards. They were droning the fourth verse when they arrived.

The bushes were splendid—densely green and speckled with rounds of pearly, light green unripe berries. In a few weeks the berries would be purple and searched after for jellies and juices. The bushes formed the border of another garden. Kate saw accurately laid out, weeded plots—carrots, peas, onions, leeks, winter cabbage, kale in perfect rows—and against the brick wall of the farmhouse a line of pink mallows.

"We'll make it a game!" Sylvia's voice rang out. "A competition."

She paired them off, a tall girl with a smaller one, a skinny one with a plump one, the athletic Frokke with the bumbling Trudy. Kate drew Ose and was content.

Now Sylvia assigned a bush to each team.

"It's speed that counts—'tough as leather, quick as a greyhound,' remember. The winners get double helpings of dessert."

"And the losers?" Kriemhild asked.

"There's always the john to scour."

The girls laughed.

"I'll be timekeeper," Sylvia said. "When I blow my whistle—"

Kate had raised her hand. "But how do I know when to stop?"

"When the bush has been completely stripped."

"But then the berries won't ripen—they'll wither."

"It's the foliage we're here to collect. We're not concerned with the berries. Understood?" Sylvia sounded very sure.

"Yes!"

The whistle shrilled. The teams dashed forward. There was a mad scramble into the cover of leaves. The tearing and ripping and plundering began. Branches were bent and broken, bark scarred. The girls sweated. The village kids stood gawking. Sylvia cheered from the sidelines.

At first, working independently, Kate and Ose grabbed for the leaves within easy reach, stuffing their bags. Later they took turns weighing down a branch to bag the green at the top. Kate heard Kriemhild wishing for the air raid siren, but it was only a dog that wailed.

The bushes were a sad ruin when they stopped. Frokke's and Marianne's teams had finished at the same time. Now the weight of their bags would decide the winner. Kate and Ose were in the upper third, and Kate was pleased. She kept her eyes on Frokke to catch her if she tried to smuggle a rock into her bag.

"The wife won't like it," was all the mayor said, ogling Sylvia, when he drove up on his tractor. He let the one prisoner hoist the twenty bags onto the cart. The guard was more voluble. "Looks like the enemy retreated, leaving nothing alive or useful," he grumbled, pacing beside the empty bushes. "Burnt earth, they call it on the Russian front. The Ivans couldn't have done it better. And don't you have more sense than to pick someone's garden? Private property."

"The Führer is asking for *everyone's* share in the effort to win the war." Sylvia confronted him, and he grinned foolishly.

"Quick, quick," he railed at the prisoner.

Sylvia told Marianne to take command; she would ride along with the mayor to see that the leaves were properly weighed and stored.

"Or there'll be twenty bags with green slime by tomorrow," Kate said. "And useless." She had seen it happen.

"Let's go swimming," Sylvia called as she rode away. The mayor had given her a cushion to sit on.

"Hurrah, swimming!"

But long before they had arrived at the swimming hole, the air raid siren struck them down. The girls vanished into a potato field.

It was comfortable in the cozy furrows. The odor of the plants was strong and bitter. Kate wondered if the fumes were poisonous. The twins did not know, and when the question had traveled all the way to Marianne, the garbled answer came back:

"My brothers' names are Fritz and Paul."

For a while the field buzzed with telephone messages and giggles. Later Kate and the girls near her watched the fat, slow clouds and invented names and guessed each other's thoughts.

"A tank!"

"No."

"A castle!" So it went.

Kate sat up when she heard the plane. The field around her sprouted heads, and for the first time that afternoon she saw Harry. She waved. And she did not duck as her comrades did when with a sudden, ear-splitting roar a single plane loomed above the tree line of the state forest. Kate watched it, spellbound. It flew so low she could distinguish its markings. It was a B 52 Flying Fortress, as her dad had taught her. It seemed intact, propellers whirling, with no sign of smoke. An American airplane. *The enemy*.

As it hovered directly above her, all Kate did was to pull her head a little between her shoulders. She was waiting for the burst of machine-gun fire, the zing of the bombs. Far away the gang of prisoners had stopped working. When she sat in the shadow of the plane, she shuddered. Nothing happened.

A gray cloud, like a mass of black flies, danced in the plane's wake. It coasted with the breeze. Westward the plane became smaller and smaller and disappeared. Fluttering, the cloud descended.

"Leaflets," cried Kate. "Enemy leaflets!"

There must have been hundreds and hundreds. She was up and running, jumping over the potato plants. The twins were leaping along, Kriemhild barefoot with her pumps in her hand, Harry following. The others waited till the all-clear. Like oversize snowflakes the leaflets came down, wavering, settling among the beets, in the tall grass of the meadow beyond, in a clump of trees, in a field of oats.

Kate saw one of the prisoners reach for one as it sailed past and let it go again. He probably couldn't read, she thought, and started gathering. Harry already had his arms full. She could see his collection grow and grow.

"Dump all the paper here! We'll burn it later." Frokke and the rest of the girls had arrived on the scene. Soon everyone, even the guards and their prisoners, were picking up leaflets, and only the papers caught high in the trees were left to fade.

With a collector's eye Kate checked through the printed sheets. There were five different leaflets, four new to her.

"Thirty-seven German U-boats sunk in May. Battle of the Atlantic lost," read a black headline.

"German morale down because of stepped-up bombing raids."

There were photographs of skeleton houses and mountains of rubble, blown-apart tiger tanks, crews in lifeboats.

Kate despised the enemy for such outrageous lies.

"Germans violate Geneva Convention on prisoners of war." This one sheet she slipped into her pocket. She would read it later, alone.

"Coming?" Harry, she knew, was heading for his dream tank.

Kate shook her head. Right now she would stay with her comrades. It felt good to be together.

Holding hands, they danced around the fire. There were any number of songs about rising flames, and they sang a couple. In the end they were hot and dusty and smeared with ashes, and the right heel of Kriemhild's pumps had finally broken off.

"Gosh, I was sure he'd machine-gun us."

"Never saw us under the potatoes."

"With one antiaircraft gun we could have knocked him down."

The girls surrounded the dying fire.

"And we could have captured the crew." This from Trudy, who bungled everything.

Kate thought of parading their prisoners into Decherow, with the mayor, the area party and youth leaders, the villagers, and the kids of the hostel awed; the proud speeches, the medals awarded. She liked the thought. All of them heroes, like Werner Grasshof.

By now it was too late for the swimming hole, and on the march back the three friends, Marianne, Inga, and Ose, developed the pump game to get cool and clean.

"It's a craze where we come from," Marianne said. "And the green is just right for it, with the pump and trough in the center. All we need are the two small portable pumps with hoses and nozzles from the school's stock."

Inga dashed off to get them.

She would ask her dad to play on his next leave, Kate thought. He would love a game with bombers and fighters attacking, trying to drop missiles on gun sites, one missile, one bomb; and antiaircraft batteries trying to ward off the enemy with gushes of water, one squirt directly into the face equivalent to blasting the cockpit to pieces. Shot-down planes and bombs delivered on target counted during rounds. Kate could already see her dad add touches of flying lore, the long elegant white scarf of the pilot, the military salute for the enemy about to crash.

Their first mission was London. Kate's group talked strategy to outsmart its defenses.

"We'll pay them back for bombing our cities," they pledged.

Kate, in the role of a fighter, took off, winged her way around the green, pounced on the gun site, veered off and swooped down again. It was fun to see the girls pump frantically and still evade the jet of water, being so much quicker than the gunners, taking aim. Kate and her two fellow fighters charged at the gun site, spiraled off, dodged and bluffed till the girls at the pumps were thoroughly confused. When at last Kate switched into a bomber and they attacked in full number, there was hardly any water and they dropped their missiles right on target. Only Sigrid got her whole head drenched and was counted out. It served her right, Kate thought. She had dumped five armfuls of rocks into the trough, barely getting her legs splashed, and felt victorious.

In the second round of the game Kate was defending Ber-

lin. Kriemhild had clambered on the shoulders of the avenging angel and was commenting on the enemy formations
approaching from the west.

"Cowardly enemy aircraft advancing, hiding behind a
bank of shady clouds," she droned on. "Take cover, civilian population!"

Chickens, ducks, dogs, and village kids had long fled.

"We'll protect Berlin with our bodies," cried Frokke,
and Kate and her comrades whooped. The other team, arms
outstretched, buzzed across the green. Kate pumped furiously, filling the trough. Other girls were manning the small
pumps and hoses.

"Nobody will pass our ring of fire!" she shouted, and
barked at Sigrid for not working fast enough, and snapped
at Frokke for aiming the hose too low. As the water squirted
into the dirt, Kate grabbed the hose. She pointed at faces,
shouted for more water pressure, called warnings, ordered
everybody to scoop water with their hands, to turn the enemy back. And they did.

No bombs were delivered, and seven bombers were shot
down.

Kriemhild broke out in a cry of "Victory!" and Kate
grinned back at Frokke.

It wasn't anybody's fault that Harry was caught between
fronts in the ensuing turmoil, Kate thought, though he was
soaked mercilessly and the first to be dunked in the trough.
Twenty hands, from both teams, held him under. But they
were all dripping wet and splotched with mud at the end,
and it was only a game, wasn't it? No need for rescue.

That night Sylvia moved back into the big classroom, right
under the picture of the Führer. The girls had sent a dele-

gation to the teachers' lounge, Frokke and Marianne and even Brunhild, to beg her to return, and they had carried her trunk in triumph.

Earlier Sylvia had told them that their camp was the first in the area to reach and surpass its goal. "They were absolutely staggered at the collection center," she had said. "There isn't enough room for a harvest like ours, but they weighed the bags, and we're way ahead of everybody else. Isn't it wonderful?"

The girls had burst into cheers.

Now Sylvia regaled them with stories of her own flights and of the Red Baron and his buddies.

Dad wouldn't recognize himself, thought Kate, and she smiled. Singing rounds on the green, she had carried the melody once against all her comrades.

NINETEEN

◇ For a couple of days it seems to me I am off-guard.

I use the stairs without imagining prints of temples.

I do not stumble over pails with sand and water, a mop or an ax on the landing.

I hear Aunt Sylvia's voice and think nothing special.

On Tuesday I'm gone all day, first to school, then to a swimming meet where we have a good chance of winning but don't. Some of my friends and I spend the late afternoon at Werner's house, listening to music, and later we drop in at a dingy coffee shop on our suburban main street. It is the hangout of the eleventh and twelfth graders, and we like to irritate the owners at least once a week. At ten o'clock all the kids under sixteen are turned out, and I slowly wander home.

I hear Aunt Sylvia in Grandma's room, and I tiptoe past to keep Bozo from reporting me. I do not want Grandma to tell me that it is a school night.

I fall asleep thinking of how to establish my own state with my own laws. A small state.

On Wednesday after school Nick and I go shopping with Mom for winter clothes. I need boots and a coat. Mom buys the coat I like best, though I can hear Grandma commenting that it won't last another year. I don't want it to last that long. In a year I will be different.

Nick wants a black leather jacket and settles for an army surplus arctic survival parka.

We reward Mom with pizza, and when we return home, Dad and Aunt Sylvia are at a movie in downtown Berlin.

Bozo sits close to me while I watch TV.

On my way up to bed I hear them come in.

"It's a wonderful movie!" pronounces Aunt Sylvia.

I take three steps at a time and shut my door. I don't want to know the story. It's a mystery and I'm planning on seeing it in a few weeks.

On Thursday I have a bad day in school. There is a surprise grammar test, and I can't find my favorite pink pen and have to work with one of Werner's chewed pencils. The test is fairly easy, but I'm still mad when I get home. I storm into the house, almost toppling Grandma.

"Who took my pen?" I shout, throwing my books into one corner and the coat into the other. "Someone in this family stole my pink pen!"

Mom comes down and without a word picks up my stuff.

I go on shouting for a while, though my mood has changed and I feel near laughter.

"Kate lacks control," observes Aunt Sylvia. "No self-discipline."

It does not touch me.

I shout into her face and stomp up to my room.

The pen is on my desk, and I burst out laughing.

Later I tell Grandma that I am sorry I upset her. I *am* sorry.

Friday morning at breakfast Dad tells one of his dreams.

Mom lingers over a third cup of coffee.

Grandma is happy with her four-and-a-half-minute egg.

Nick does his math homework.

Aunt Sylvia moves about the kitchen busily. Listening to Dad makes her restless.

It is getting very late for school, but I don't want to interrupt Dad. His dreams interest me. On other days he will gravely puzzle over one of mine.

Today his dream is a nightmare, full of murderous chases across the Berlin airport, Tempelhof, among screaming sirens and flashing lights and moving luggage carousels.

"We thread in and out of airplanes and dart along their wings," he says. "I'm with a boy I admired a lot back in school—a tough guy with a medal for saving someone's life. The shadows are hounding us . . . beasts . . . men . . . I don't know what. He races ahead and I follow and he seems to be getting smaller. When I finally catch up with him at the end of the runway, he has shrunk to nothing. Nothing! Then I woke up thinking, how glorious, now I can make new friends."

Dad sees the clock above the corner cupboard, and he looks guilty. "Gosh, kids, it's terribly late. Come on, I'll give you a ride to school."

"I'll drive them." Aunt Sylvia reaches for Mom's car keys.

"No," I say. "I'll go with Dad. With all his practice during the night, he'll be quicker."

TWENTY

🦋 *July 8, 9, and 10, 1943*

Thursday and Friday were packed with regular camp activities, though no more grazing, as Sylvia called the picking of medicinal plants. There were rehearsals in the morning, swimming in the afternoon, music and Sylvia's tales at night. No drills, but lavish flag ceremonies with poems and songs and solemn promises to country and Führer.

The village kids stopped staring and were digging a patch of early potatoes near the Gatow road. There were no more thefts reported, and Olga went on cooking and serving and washing up, mute and aloof, with the girls on kitchen duty watching her. A large continental high was keeping the sky blue except for a few ponderous, unhurried clouds, not even sullied by enemy planes. On Wednesday night Kate had heard the wail of the siren and then a drowsy Sylvia telling them to go back to sleep, which she had done.

Kate was almost happy.

First, Sylvia had summoned her to raise the flag on Thursday morning and had commended her for her part in yesterday's game.

"I was told," Sylvia said, "that you threw yourself into the fight with great courage, inspired your comrades, and caused your team to win—an example for all of us."

Erect, Kate had looked straight ahead and had felt her heart beating faster.

Second, there had never been a repeat of the magic act. Frokke, the assistant, knew nothing about it. Kate had seen no props, and she had nearly persuaded herself that Sylvia had canceled the show. Maybe her sister had realized she wasn't good enough. Or she had relented, Kate thought.

Lighthearted, she went through the steps of the Maypole dance, each practice run ending in a complete and hilarious muddle with the colorful ribbons bunched in a snarl. Frokke had asked her to join the dancers. And Kate listened to the recorder group and hummed with the singers. She laughed hard at the twins' skit where Kate's only task was to carry a pail of water onstage with a dead-pan face, and she got applause for expanding her role by putting the pail in Kriemhild's path, with Kriemhild avoiding it again and again until the very last moment.

"That's wonderful, Kate."

"The perfect touch."

Her comrades beamed.

Up in the attic, after minding their drying harvest, Kate wrote in her notebook that she liked summer camp a lot.

Ose had shown her how to do a back flip at the swimming hole, and she had mastered it quickly.

Marianne had asked her to come and visit her right after camp.

Inga had taught everyone the call of the golden oriole and the wood thrush.

Sigrid had sewn the seam of her skirt and washed.

Kriemhild had unbent and was wearing her second pair

of shoes instead of the horrible pumps. Now she was very fast on her feet.

Brunhild had begun talking when her twin was absent.

Frokke had shared half an enormous sausage.

Not a word about Harry.

When he sidled up to Kate Thursday afternoon, whispering about Glashagen Spring and some urgent, secret business and wanted her to come along, Kate shook her head brusquely. She and the other girls were hanging around the war memorial, waiting for supper.

"Your special friend! What does he want from you?" Kriemhild inquired.

"I don't like creeps," Marianne said.

"How can you stand him, coming so close?" someone said. "He looks disgusting."

"The village idiot." Sylvia dismissed him.

Nobody paid any attention when Kate defended Harry with a rather meek-sounding, "You know he isn't."

Soon they chased one another inside. Kate did not see Harry all evening.

On Friday morning she watched him push his wheelbarrow across the green. It was stacked high with baskets of apples. He had delivered five of them at the school—cool-tasting, lime-green, tart early summer apples.

"Look at all the beautiful fruit!" Kriemhild smacked her lips. "I love pears."

"Apples," Frokke corrected.

"I don't love apples." Kriemhild grinned. "Pears are my favorite fruit."

There was laughter, and they all followed Harry's course

from the stage, where they had been rehearsing another folk dance.

"Bumbling idiot," Sylvia said as the wheelbarrow tipped, spilling the apples. The girls clapped.

It looked very funny. Harry had let go of the handles to grab the first slipping basket, and the wheelbarrow had plomped down and toppled sideways. There he was on all fours, chasing after his apples among the dogs, chickens, and ducks, dusting the apples, polishing them on his shirt and pants. It looked like an accident, but Kate was absolutely sure he had upset the wheelbarrow on purpose. She became very interested.

"Bumbling idiot," Sylvia repeated.

Right then the gang of prisoners trotted onto the green, nearly trampling the apples. They stopped. Commands were shouted, and while the guards stood aside, bored, the prisoners, too, scampered in the dirt after the apples. Kate observed at least two of the prisoners slipping apples inside their rags. If Harry had wanted to pass food to them, he couldn't have planned it any better. Or even a message, she thought coolly.

"Back to practice, everybody," Sylvia called, and Kate resumed her place in the circle between Inga and the talkative twin.

Saturday began ominously. Kate woke up out of a dream suffused with apple-green light to her sister's air warden voice, grimly denouncing the thieving scum of Decherow. Four more loaves of bread, their breakfast ration, were missing, and she had banned Olga from the kitchen. "I demand from all of you extreme vigilance," she said, stamping her foot. There was ghastly soup on the table, tepid sweetened boiled milk with lumps and sticky skin. Ose and Inga were named temporary cooks, with Trudy as helper.

"Dumb Polish cow," said Frokke. "What does she want with four loaves?"

"What does anyone want with that much bread?"

"Feed it to his pigs."

"But that's a crime, squandering scarce food."

Kate was choking on her first spoonful. She could and did imagine Harry lurking behind the war memorial and pilfering the four loaves the moment Olga went to get the milk next door—another treasure for his Glashagen hideout. There was Sylvia's flashlight and Sigrid's mess kit, the flat cake, the sausage, the mayor's peas and carrots and potatoes, the stack of unexamined stuff inside the temple. It made her feel cold and apprehensive. She coughed and got up from the table. The soup was too horrible, anyway.

The mayor had dumped a wagon load of freshly cut crowns of birches outside. Kate and the twins and Frokke began to deck the stage, the barren green, the brick walls of the buildings with dewy branches, and they tied a bouquet to the top of the Maypole.

"This is wonderful!" Sylvia no longer sounded severely official.

"You really think so?" Released, all the girls plunged into the final preparations for the afternoon.

Under Sylvia's direction the stage and the green were redecorated, bunches of birch rearranged, bunting hung once more. Crews sprinkled the ground to keep the dirt down; others began raking, in a fancy pattern. Guards were posted at the roads and lanes. Kate was stationed at the entrance of the state forest road, trying to stave off the locals and their lifestock. An army truck rumbled past. Two peasant women, rakes on their shoulders, went home for lunch. Chickens scratched in the dirt. Kate, on the lookout for Harry, saw him appear between the barns opposite and vanish up the lime tree. She waved, but he did not seem to notice her. So she ran over.

"You stole our bread," she accused him.

"I need it." He was perched comfortably above her. "I'll tell you about it later. I think you'll understand."

And Kate strolled back to her corner, thinking that she would.

Then twelve head of cattle, cemented in dung, marched slowly past her toward the trough, and she was absolutely helpless. No amount of noise or commotion impressed the animals. They were not to be stopped on their way to the water. Here they drank and drank, pushing and shoving each other and messing up the tract around the trough.

"Get them off!" Sylvia ordered.

"Sh . . . move on . . . please move on!" Kate clapped her hands and gestured.

The cattle ventured toward the stage and began munching the foliage. The girls pushed against layers of dung. The animals did not budge. Sylvia waved a red skirt. Frokke kicked at a flank.

"We need whips."

"No whips." Harry, all of a sudden among them, grabbed hold of the oldest, dirtiest cow, and she followed him amiably. Ten other cows trailed her. Kate made up the rear, urging the twelfth one on. She was a stubborn beast, and Kate had to leap right and left, feign and block to keep her in line. She must look ridiculous, Kate realized when she heard the girls' laughter—an inept clown.

Sylvia called her back just before she rounded the corner.

"It's a good thing your special friend drove them off before the dumb animals wrecked everything—we want to look good this afternoon, don't we?" she said. "Though it was quite a funny sight."

Kate saw that her sister was far from amused. And Sylvia was not going to be content merely to look good. Sylvia wanted to come in first.

"There's hardly any damage," Kate said, looking straight at Sylvia. "The cows were thirsty, that's all."

"We'd better prevent Kate from doing more harm." Sylvia had turned to the other girls. "Imagine pigs dancing on the stage."

So Kate was banished inside the building.

"I want everything spick-and-span," declared her untidy sister. "Not the tiniest bit of straw in the aisle. No smudges on the blackboards. As if the Führer personally were going to inspect the camp. There'll be important visitors."

TWENTY-ONE

◊ It is the weekend Mom and Dad take off and leave us in the care of Aunt Sylvia. It, too, is a tradition, although Nick and I long ago outgrew the need to be looked after at all hours. During the rest of the year Mrs. Malek is on call when Mom and Dad are absent.

"Have a wonderful time," Aunt Sylvia calls to them from the front steps. "Don't worry! We'll get along fine, won't we?" She cradles Bozo, almost strangling him. Her words are just a formality. Usually my parents do not worry. But last night I asked them if I could come with them.

"You always loved the weekends with your aunt! You and Nick talk about nothing else for weeks afterward but the fun you had," said Mom. I thought she sounded jealous.

"Aunt Sylvia will be hurt," Dad said. "Besides, it's business, and you'd be bored."

Later Mom came to my room.

"Something's bothering you. Can I help, Kate?" She was squeezing my shoulder.

"Not now."

"Will you let me know?"

I nodded.

Now Mom does look worried, and I smile to reassure her. Dad thinks it's one of my adolescent quirks.

"What shall we do?" asks my aunt in her most conspiratorial manner when their cab pulls away from the curb. Grandma Hofmann, Nick, Aunt Sylvia, and I are waving. Bozo yaps.

I know Nick wants to go to his room and listen to music. There's a rock concert on the radio he plans to tape.

Grandma has invited a few of her old cronies: two military widows with exemplary postures; fat, rich Mrs. Weber from across the street, and a shriveled general whose monocle fascinates me. She wants Aunt Sylvia to fetch vases for the flowers, preside at her table, pour the coffee, cut the cake, and entertain. The Machu Picchu story will be a hit. I know Aunt Sylvia wants an unforgettable weekend, worthy of the preceding ones: the all-night hide-and-seek party with our friends in the darkened house; the costume session two years ago; the rocking chair contest, which I won by rocking for 14 hours, 42 minutes, and 56 seconds, beating my friend Werner by more than an hour, Nick by 15 minutes, and Grandma Hofmann by 3 minutes and 56 seconds. I had rocked from seven o'clock sharp on Saturday evening till 9:42.56 on Sunday morning, with a bathroom break every three hours.

"Let's have a séance!" I say. My voice trembles. My plan upsets me. I am no longer sure about it. Still, I want to get it over with.

Aunt Sylvia has brought a Ouija board as this year's family gift from California, and so far we have played once at Grandma's low table, with candles flickering. Mom had to be persuaded to write down the letters as they showed up under the small window of the planchette; she would have no other part in it. Grandma had put on a face like in church, and most of her rings. They had glinted in the candlelight. Nick had murmured, "Bullshit," but he had kept his fingers on the planchette. I had been intrigued and skeptical, then a lot less skeptical when the wooden planchette skitted and danced on the three legs across the board.

"Who is there?" Aunt Sylvia had sounded quite serious.

Whoever had or had not been there, we had had no chance to find out. Dad had wrecked the session by forcing the planchette to spell out "Santa Claus." None of us had thought it funny, but it inspired my plan.

"Let's have a séance!" I repeat, and Grandma Hofmann and Nick and Aunt Sylvia are enthusiastic.

After supper I am keyed up. Nick looks bleary from his rock music. Bozo, banished to the kitchen, lets out small moans. The candles are burning, and the odor of anise and polish is intense. Grandma and Aunt Sylvia's dresses rustle silkily.

I figured there are two ways to cheat—by manipulating the planchette and rearranging what it points to. So I make them enlist me to call out and write down the yesses and no's and numbers and letters.

My voice shakes properly. I am out to jolt Aunt Sylvia.

Grandpa Hofmann is the first spirit to speak up, and I swear I do nothing to influence his answers but report what takes place on the Ouija board. It is eerie.

Grandpa is in a jolly mood and again in the company of the Red Baron, as he tells us proudly. He vanishes as quickly as he did in real life when he closed the door to his study.

Grandma Hofmann sobs for a few seconds.

We wait in silence.

Then there are a number of spirits. The board twitches, the planchette squeaks, flying across it. Aunt Sylvia urges them to come forward.

"Who are you? Who is there? Talk to us!"

I throw out names. "Maren, Frokke, Marianne, Kriemhild, harelipped Harry."

"Do I know you?" Aunt Sylvia asks, bemused and yet quite calm.

"1943,1943,1943,19—" I know I get louder and louder.

"1943,19—" She looks brightly around our circle for help.

"Camp Decherow." I spell it, shouting each letter.

"The names mean nothing. You must be wrong," Aunt Sylvia says firmly. I see her wide, merry face, and I am struck by the feeling that she no longer matters to me. At some time during her visit I must have made up my mind to stop caring. She has shrunk to nothing, much like the person in Dad's dream.

"H...I...T...L..." I break off and leave the room. I do not want to call up the other Kate as a witness to be slaughtered a second time. That I came so close distresses me.

TWENTY-TWO

🐦 *July 10, 1943*

And there were visitors.

Kate watched them arrive from the attic window, where she had puttered around the plants. And she saw that Harry was watching them too. His visored cap peeked through the leaves. So he had gone back to his former post.

First came the unimportant guests—the kids from the village and their friends and dogs, the older peasants, carrying kitchen chairs and planting them in front of the stage. The boys and girls from the hostel entered the green in formation, singing, dressed in their uniforms, flags flying. Kate could see Sylvia darting from group to group, impressing on them the importance of order. Their standard-bearers were directed to the left side of the war memorial. On its right two girls of her group stood frozen, clutching their flags. The green was swarming, the pattern of her comrades' rakes no longer noticeable. The peasants were stamping it down. A truck full of soldiers braked on the state forest road, and they rambled into the green. Sylvia settled most of them on the mayor's wagon. The older guard, for once without his rifle, was slouched against a far barn wall. Kate wondered idly if the prisoners would slow down their hoeing with only one guard watching.

She could see behind the stage. There was the Maypole, the giant picture of Adolf Hitler for the final scene, the bunch of wild flowers, the recorders, a pail of water, a wreath to place at the war memorial. Count on Sylvia to do things right, Kate thought. Then she discovered a basket with magic props, partly hidden under the steps to the stage. It gave her a jolt. Her sister was going right ahead. I've been fooling myself, Kate thought angrily.

Her own group was clustered left of the stage, Sylvia now its very center, talking, giving last-minute instructions, radiant. Everybody's eyes were glued to her. Kate played with the idea of remaining where she was and watching the whole spectacle from above; she felt that removed.

Then Harry's actions caught her eye. He had slid down the tree, and from behind the trunk he seemed to be counting the soldiers on and near the wagon. Then he wiggled around groups of people, stopped to talk with two or three village kids, glided on through the crowd. He circled the stage and her own group, as if searching for her; he even looked up at the school building. Finally he disappeared into the state forest road. He was up to something, thought Kate, and it must be important or he wouldn't miss the show.

"Well, here you are, Kate! I hunted all over for you." It was Kriemhild at the top of the stairs. "You weren't thinking of deserting Brunhild and me, were you? Or the doomed Maypole dance? Trudy'll ruin it if nobody else does."

Kate let herself be drawn back. Her comrades were counting on her, but the earlier feeling of easy camaraderie was gone.

So she was waiting in a leaf-green skirt with the other dancers near the stage when the most important visitors arrived. First the long snout of a staff car pushed onto the green. A number of high-ranking officers climbed out and strutted toward the war memorial. Here they regrouped, eyeing their surroundings. Kate did not see Werner Grasshof. Then the mayor plowed through the crowd and was offered one of the front-row chairs. He sat down heavily. Just when Sylvia was about to open the show, the people were again stirred up. A passage was formed to let four Hitler Youth leaders advance on the stage.

It was a delegation from the area office. Kate recognized the woman who had installed her sister. She was accompanied by another girl and two young men, all of them spruced up in faultless uniforms and a number of badges.

Sylvia flew forward to report.

"Heil Hitler! Twenty girls of Camp Decherow are present to entertain the people of the village!"

The woman leader addressed all of them—Sylvia, the girls, and their guests. She talked of doing one's duty on the home front, poured praise over Sylvia, lauding her record and a particularly outstanding deed. "It's a sacred obligation to accomplish any task the Führer assigns to you," she said. "But Sylvia has done far more than was asked of her." Kate found herself glowing with her sister and thinking of the glider flight, the rescue of bombing victims out of a crumbling flaming house, something heroic, and felt deflated when it boiled down to twenty bags of damp foliage. She nearly laughed.

"A lot of green slime! What a fraud!" she muttered as they filed onstage after the accolade. But she could not have explained what or whom she meant.

Their first folk song, done by all of them together, sounded strong and fresh.

Then came the dance.

At best there was a brief muddle in each Maypole dance. Sylvia, holding the pole upright, was directing the steps of the dancers. In peasant frocks and white blouses, ten of the girls whirled around her, each clinging to one of the red, blue, green, or yellow satin ribbons and weaving them all into an intricate pattern. All the girls were singing, and the audience burst heartily into the refrain.

At first everything went well. Kate hopped along, following Inga's lead and checking on the pattern above. Then someone blundered. As the strips snarled up and got shorter and shorter, the dancing became more frantic. The girls reeled around till all of a sudden they were tied to the pole like so many Indians to a stake.

"Idiots!" hissed Sylvia, caught among them. "Let go and bow!"

Just as the people were changing from singing to open-mouthed staring to the first faint giggles, the dancers rushed forward, curtsied, reached once more for their satin ribbons, and executed a perfect dance to roaring applause. Count on Sylvia to turn back disaster, Kate thought.

Someone recited a poem about the German farmer.

The recorders piped across the green.

When Frokke, flushed with pride, announced the magic show, Kate walked off. She was going to watch her sister's much-touted performance from a distance, surrounded by strangers. Here she admitted jealousy.

There was a hum of excitement over the green.

And the people loved Sylvia. Dazzling them, she spun through her magic acts. There were more blunders than before.

"Oops!" she said. "There it goes! Can't win them all!" as a coin rolled on the ground.

"It looks as if one of you filched four aces," she reproached her audience when all the mayor's pockets turned out to be empty. Frokke, ignored, was passing new coins and cards to Sylvia.

There were calls of "Not bad," and "Marvelous!" A kid squealed, and the soldiers grinned broadly. Kate looked for Harry but could not find him. She missed his company.

Then Sylvia got ready for her big mind-reading act, answering questions although they were hidden away in sealed envelopes. As she explained, people in the audience began to print and scribble. Frokke collected the stuffed and sealed envelopes, looking smug. She's been briefed, thought Kate, and she could not help feeling envious. It had always been her role.

Kate watched as her sister swooned, magnificent in a blue bedspread. Frokke, bowing, offered the first white paper. It was raised high, shown all around, and while the spectators gaped in awed silence, Sylvia pressed it against her forehead. She seemed to have fallen into a deep trance, pulling the people along.

That was when a motorcycle buzzed along the state forest road and screeched to a stop on the green. The driver, a young soldier, jumped off, sprinted to the group of officers, and reported. There were urgent, unintelligible staccato sounds.

Everybody had become very much interested. The soldiers on the wagon stood up straight. The mayor rose slowly; the people had turned away from the stage; the uniformed boys and girls craned their necks. Sylvia, still grasping the envelope, stepped to the edge of the stage. Kate saw that the officers' faces were no longer relaxed and friendly, but resolute. It was very quiet. One of them leaped up next to Sylvia.

"People of Decherow! There has been a breakout of prisoners of war. It is everybody's duty to assist in their recapture." His voice was strident.

"How many of the bastards are at large?" grumbled the mayor.

"A work party of six prisoners has not returned on time," was the answer. "We need more information. One of their guards is confused, and the second one is missing."

For a moment there was hushed silence. Sylvia had let go of the envelope, and it fluttered toward the mayor. Irritated, he slapped it down. Kate quickly looked for the elderly soldier and saw him, staring dumbfounded up at the officer. She thought of the gang of prisoners she had seen so often and of Harry and the stockpile at Glashagen Spring. Suddenly she knew why he had needed the four loaves of bread; in fact, he had needed six.

Now orders were barked. The staff car roared off. The soldiers reboarded the truck; the Youth Hostel kids marched away from the green. The mayor spoke of search parties, and the crowd broke up quietly. Soon the green was empty except for Kate and her comrades, a few village kids, and Sylvia in her magic robe.

Kate watched her sister lean forward. There was a gleam in Sylvia's eyes, and for a moment she looked smugly

147◇

satisfied. Kate knew Sylvia was seeing herself handing over the prisoners of war to a stunned and grateful authority.

"Come closer." Her sister beckoned, and the group huddled below her. "Wouldn't it be great if we recaptured the prisoners! Just imagine us doing it!" She was radiating such enthusiasm that everybody was spellbound. It would be an opportunity to look good, to come out ahead, the ultimate triumph, thought Kate.

Now, probing and urgent, Sylvia searched face after face. "They would need civilian clothing, provisions, a place to hide and store them—in short someone from the outside who knows his way around—a thief, a traitor—"

She stopped and studied Kate.

And Kate thought of Harry as he spoke of saving the chunk of cake for his friends.

"What do you know about the harelipped kid who's always snooping around?" Sylvia asked lightly. "Your special friend, Kate!"

"Harry is all right," Kate said resolutely. She was suddenly quite sure she would not let him be sacrificed for another of Sylvia's triumphs. Like Maren, or the boy from the Youth Hostel, the elderberry bushes, or . . . The list was far too long. And she liked Harry.

"I thought I could depend on you." Sylvia frowned, puzzled and apparently hurt. "You're refusing to help."

Sylvia turned away to the village kids and told them to think hard about any possible hiding place. It would not take her long to worm out a memory of Glashagen Spring. Suddenly she swung back to Kate.

"You and that harelipped kid were together an awful lot!" Sylvia's voice was sharp, demanding obedience.

"Where were you? Where is he now?"

Someone sniggered nervously; the others stared at Kate, hardly breathing.

"I'll never tell you." Kate defied her sister. "Never."

Then she ran to warn Harry.

"You know they won't get away," she heard Sylvia call after her. "We'll hunt you down!"

TWENTY-THREE

Kate Hofmann was shot dead on the evening of July 10, 1943, at Glashagen Spring by military police. They took her for one of the fugitives, but the prisoners of war were long gone, and I hope they are safe. Kate was shot in the head.

Harry Overbek

Harry must have sat a long time next to her working on this message, I think and look at the stiff, carefully drawn letters. It is the final entry in the other Kate's slate-blue notebook. She came to warn him, and I like to think she came to warn the prisoners, too, though that is my version of Kate's story. She ends hers by racing away from the green.

I close the notebook and lock it in my desk. I have decided what to do. I owe it to Kate and myself and maybe even to Aunt Sylvia. She will be in her room after the broken-up séance.

"I know what happened to your sister Kate at Camp Decherow," I will say to Aunt Sylvia. "I have read the other Kate's diary." The words will scratch my throat, but I no longer care about her answer.

About the Author

T. Degens is the author of the highly praised *Transport 7-41-R,* winner of the first IRA Children's Book Award and the Horn Book Award, and an ALA Notable Book. Her most recent book for Viking is *Friends.* Ms. Degens lives in Hamburg, Germany.